CAN HE OUTRUN HIS OWN PAST?

ECHOES OF THE MOOR

A NOVEL

RISHI UPPAL

INDIA • SINGAPORE • MALAYSIA

ISBN 979-8-88521-478-0

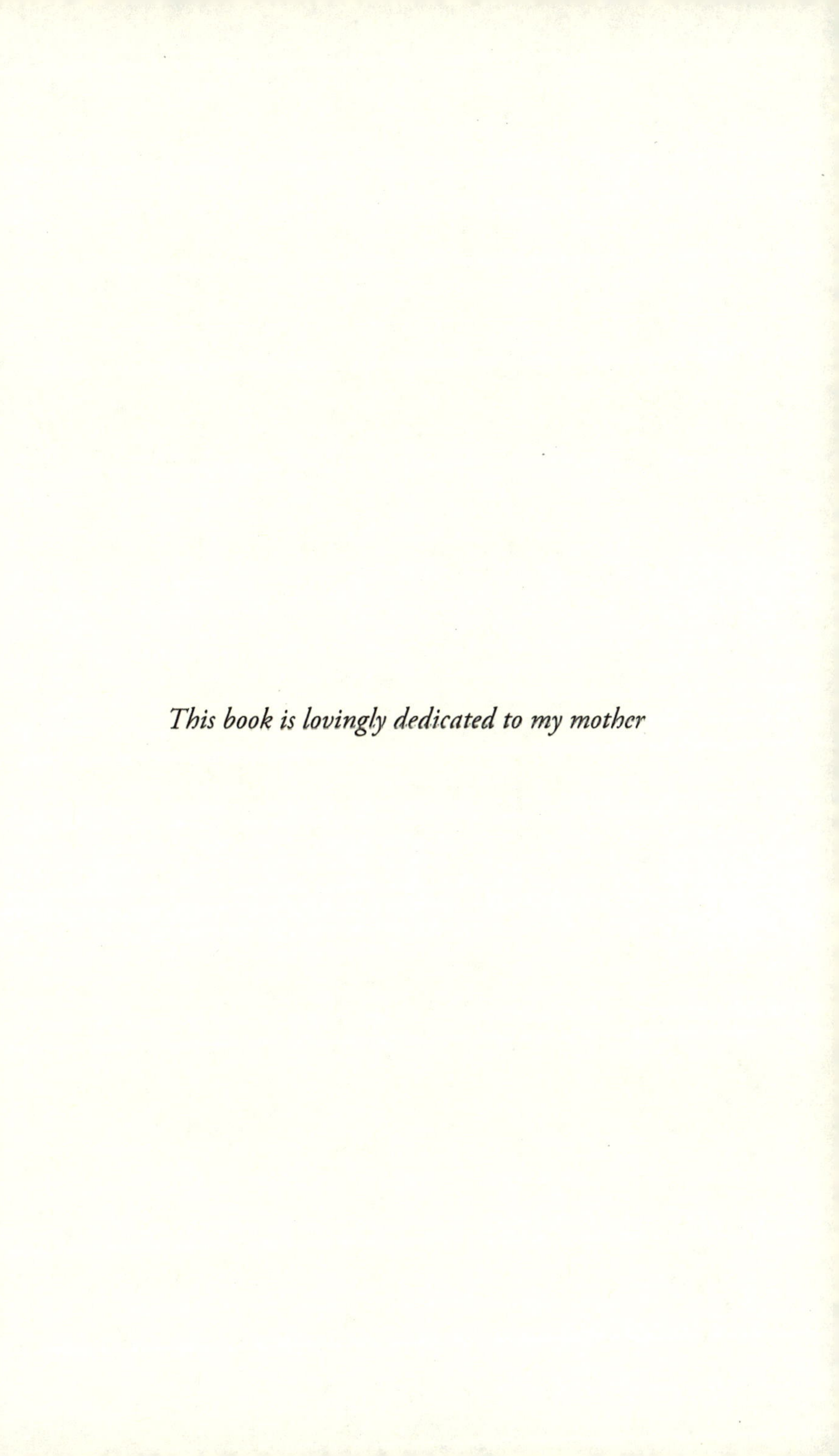

This book is lovingly dedicated to my mother

Part One

I

Gulping down the *morcel*, a little boy watched, tiny brown eyes glued to the human figure next to his bed. His mother was squatting on her haunches, actively seeking, trying to dive farther into the stockpile of wardrobes. He was observing the action in anticipation. She twisted around and smirked, turning over a black tattered leather pouch in the open. He clapped in drama and affection.

She held her arms backwards and moved towards him, then drawing forward both of her palms, she asked, "Which hand is it in?" He stared at her palms and again at her eyes. That was his most preferred game. Lifting her eyebrows, she suggested he make a choice between the hands.

Thinking for a moment, he touched the fist on the right, and with love she freed the fist and lent him the present. A key fob finished in solid wooden brown colour, in the carving of a doe with a key ring affixed to it. It was a good luck charm.

"That's your Christmas present, my son," she said.

He felt the four limbs of the doe. She smiled at his astonishment and aided him to see the name. He could figure out the legs were the alphabets written on the designed piece, and it says his name 'Renil'. The most precious gift he would ever hold, prepared on personal request for him. The craft company G&M was special in the way of their craft and log keeping and true masters of customized items. No matter how minor the sold craft, it invariably passed to the records as an established practice. They also shared a copy with the shopper as proof of receipt and reminder.

She was his world, a best friend, an ally, a source of strength and his teacher. The mother and son giggled in the place as the sunlight gently settled. A pleasant aroma of curry lingering in the air reminded her of the pot on the boiler, and shortly it was time for supper.

The middle-aged man in the other room concluded his local bottle of whisky and didn't care about what day it was. All the days were the same for him and so was Christmas of year 96.

After putting the plate on the coffee-cum-dinner table, she rushed out of the smoke-filled room as quickly as she could, without eye contact. Almost about to enter the kitchen, she heard a smack on the table followed by her name called upon in an annoyed tone, "Rokaya, come here, you bitch!"

Suddenly, she could not move, filled with horror and monotonous feeling. It felt as if someone was choking her. Her heart was racing, and all she wished to do was curl up into a ball and wait for someone to shield her. But no one would.

Consuming more than he could bear and thereafter criticizing his loss at the gambling to her, she learnt the trouble was looking at her in the face. Frustration and distilled ethanol is an adequate blend to make for an irate man. Uncontrollable after the liquor worked inside of him, thrashing up his wife was the resort to discharge his sentiments. Renil knew what was coming next. He recognized the tones – the lash meant the belt; the cries meant pounding and moaning – rape.

Helpless, staring in the dark, bolted into his room. He always assumed someday the nuisance would end. He kept brushing his key ring as if it was some wishing lamp, in the hope for some genie to come and save the day while his mother was being mercilessly abused in the room across the wall, but maybe such a miracle was never to happen.

Darkness was his companion and false hopes, his lullaby to sleep. His mother never retaliated, never even lifted her tone and never uttered a word against it. She believed the boy looked up to her, and she had taught him that the test of a religion is not religiousness but love and forgiveness.

'Sweet child, those who cannot hold their stress with grace attack the gentle nature. It makes you a victim now; will make you great in a lifetime. Through sadness we learn empathy, to realize how others feel in pain; it transforms us and makes us all kinder.'

But secretly she wept tears of blood, searching within herself. What did she do to deserve all this?

II

As the years flew by, conditions remained untouched. The clock hanging at the same unwashed wall for the last thirteen years moved tick-tock, tick-tock and then without pause, it slammed into reverse. A man turns into what he thinks about all day, so he became troubled, nothing new about the effect of time on the human mind, especially on the children growing up.

He remained lost and dazed, sitting on the cracked stairs, looking at the rough and shaggy grass of the lawn. He kept tossing his good luck key chain in the air and grabbing it back, wondering should he intervene or leave his father to his matters alone? The most compelling part of growing is a realization that you can always save the ones you love. And because he was becoming strong with age, his thoughts pondered upon the former. This was what his mind told him, but his heart, the one that adhered to the words of his mother, always insisted on the latter.

He encountered the youth rush, and the blood boils, rage and the anger he felt within got exerted on the walls of his room every evening. To avoid unbearable noise coming from the other room and to dispose of his emotions, he hit on the walls as if they were punching bags, leaving the hands mostly bruised and bloody but his mind at peace.

Gone too weak to take the beating after all these years, his mother was presumably unconscious within minutes of the door pushed on him and with time the hasp lock got reduced to just an hour, on several occasions only a few minutes.

Once unlatched, it seemed as if a war had paused. An injured soldier is being pulled back to the bunker. The cuts and bruises were always fresh as new but with the same old lifelessness of the human body that he called mother. When band-aiding her cuts and wounds, he used to see his bruises, and the only gratification he could find in the affair.

Utter darkness and silence embraced the house, and the mother and son rotted in the tenebrous. But the darkroom was like a place out of time, a place to rest without consequences, a place to recharge and forget the things that happened. Renil had adjusted to dark completely. He was the man nurse to his mother, and to patch up her wounds he had to work in the ill-lit setup.

III

Even though the classroom walls were bare, the windows were wide, or at least they seemed to be when the lunch break was nearing, the lessons poured out from the teacher in the same dull standard it had for the past fifteen years. The bell rang, and he closed his notebooks, waiting impatiently for the willow-wand-stick-like teacher to leave. She handed out homework as usual before leaving, without caring much if the class would do it or not.

If it hadn't been for his maternal uncle's generous financial aid, he could never afford education.

Shortly after the teacher walked out of the class, everyone left for lunch except for Renil. He held his partner's hand and urged him to stay around for a little longer. The young curly-haired boy named Cyrus complied and remained at the spot until the classroom was reduced to just the two. Dragging the bag from his right, he settled it on the wooden top in solitude and pointed his partner in crime to sneak peek into his schoolbag.

"What is that?" Cyrus asked curiously.

A small transparent bottle unveiled from the cover of crumbled newspaper packing, it had white sachets in it. Taking a pill out from its sachet, he crammed it down.

"Do you wish to try?"

"Are you sure?" his friend asked hesitatingly.

"Come on, Cyrus! Don't act stupid."

Eager to prove his smartness, he took one of the small, round white pills.

"Come on now, let's go."

The sun was mild, and the air was cool. Some boys were playing basketball on the court. Making their way through the stairs, they crossed the school garden and turned around the corner, moving to the food mess.

For a few minutes waiting along the side-line reaching the basketball court, they followed the brownish-orange ball with black ribs. It started from the baseline and changing hands reached the centre, then it got passed from the centre of the court to the feeder who was wearing the blue hoopster jersey. He jumped and threw the ball towards the opposite baseline where his teammate received it, judging by his speed and reflexes – the power forward.

The crew-cut boy was athletic, and before he could get screened or blocked, he was on his way to the lay-up shot. The ball leaving his hands smoothly bounced at the board before making its way through the basket. But it all felt like a slow-motion replay to them.

Renil pushed Cyrus back in the moment and the party started again, passing the boys who were celebrating their score. The two went on and crossed the gates to the Food Hall when Cyrus told his buddy to carry on.

He asked, "What's wrong?"

Cyrus was quiet but his lips were mumbling. Smiling back at his friend, he said, "Nothing, go on, I'll see you in a minute."

Renil shrugged and marched alone to the arbitrary walking path of the meal-serving counter inside the Food Hall of John Adams.

IV

A long face looked both young and old at the same time. He had prominent cheekbones and a well-defined chin and nose. His face tells of the lean body beneath. Round glasses covered the solid black eyes which were staring at him, the expression serious but not unkind. The hands were slowly coming close to each other, and the face was stretching from the eyebrows. The authority in the voice sounded familiar as if he knew who the speaker was. Renil blinked his eyes in continuity but could not surmise.

'We have no tolerance for such behaviour,' the voice replayed in his head like in a daydream.

The sound of teenagers chatting was a little louder than usual.

'Silly me, I am crazy,' he thought.

In awe, he continued to stare at the sight. The slow-motion drama went on, like the one never seen before. Going closer, he tried again, and at that moment a sound of clap alerted him back to his senses.

We have no tolerance for such behaviour, Renil, the harsh words given to him by the provost. He was at the school assembly section, still in the aftermath of the white pill.

Found motionless in the bathroom by the school janitor, Cyrus got shifted from the medical room to the nearby hospital, eventually. Everybody had pointed the finger at the one who shared his bench, and the teacher frisked his schoolbag. They found a vial wrapped in a newspaper. The label on the outside of the bottle had a tiny red coloured disclaimer – Contains drugs; use only if prescribed.

He was being shamed in front of the entire school for all good reason, and they kept the assembly to ensure the message of zero tolerance to drugs reached all the students. But he was too young to consider all of it.

They made repeated calls to his parents, but nobody answered. Since no one took liability for the boy, they removed him in the last year of his schooling.

His mother was too feeble to attend his teacher meetings; his father had gone broke to put a plate for him on the table; the sum of money his uncle gave them had drained, and for him, he was too demented to face the reality. Not sure of what the future holds, he gave up on the idea of formal education and involved more with the boys from the streets. They jostled and banged for the best seats on the park bench, taunted each other endlessly, competed to see who could spit farther, drink beer faster or belch the loudest. Ideal parents advise their kids to stay away from these boys.

He turned into a street hawker within weeks of his new company. To segregate the chemicals and catalysts as per their demand in the boulevard, he learnt to push the sale. The dealing of hallucinogen was simple to understand – the more you could sell, the higher your number of shoppers; the more often they come back to you, the better your chances of earning and survival. As he learnt to sustain, he climbed his way to authorities and access.

With exposure to street fights, he had learnt the basics of body-to-body combat and also learnt how to use household weapons like wooden sticks, trash cans and wooden bats. The vicious circle he got pushed into trained him how to steal and deceive people, secretly developing a syndrome defined as manic depression. His need for sleep diminished, and he was turning into an agitated young man who ended up in fights.

He was far from help.

V

Under the moonlight, the avenue lay still with neatly mown grass banks and well-manicured young and matured trees, almost woodland look. Beneath their boughs were cars parked on both sides. The main exit offered a beautiful panoramic view.

The duplex washed in the tinge of blue stood opposite the park, shoulder to shoulder with the group of mahogany trees. Its stairs painted pearl white matched cleverly with the asphalt that stretched unbroken for miles. The four white stairs leading to an enormous door were the access to the interiors of the establishment, and the platform between the door and the stairs was the small porch.

The inhabitants of the duplex were a family of three, an organized and reputed man, Mr Victor Anthony, his wife, Demica, who was a librarian at the council library and their son, Ervin.

Nothing was ever a problem for Mr Anthony. Everyone was his friend. He slid effortlessly into social groups, be it sports, politics or education. He was quiet, but not out of shyness. It was like a conscious choice of being reserved to observe before getting involved with something. He worked hard, got his work done. He spent mornings attending yoga sessions at his neighbours, followed by a good read through the daily newspaper and desk work thereafter. As punctual as a veteran, disciplined and followed everything by the hands of the clock from morning till bedtime.

The evening stroll post-dinner was his treasured part of the day. All by himself, like the flora, alive and unseeing, enjoying the breeze, he used to warble his favourite songs while walking down Parkview Street.

The road he went majorly served as the access to the mahogany park and was quieter during this time of the late evening. His walking style defined authority and the posture was perfect, his hands placed behind his back, holding one another.

Strolling in the direction opposite of the road, he curved around from the first block back for his home. Completing his stroll, he felt someone following him. He turned immediately to assure but found no one. Adjusting his eyeglasses, he continued.

VI

The smoke twisted in its artistic way, forming curls in the gloom, illuminated by the bar lights. Tavern, loud music, bar food, chips, a jangle of voices saying, "To luck", a hand raised the toast and others followed. Successive rounds of alcohol heavily influenced the jokes, laughter and talking noise. They celebrated most of the evenings, and the recent rampage had called for special sedation.

He opened the chest button of his white colour linen shirt, allowing it to loosen up. To describe his appearance at this moment would miss the point. It was already half-past nine. He was drunk, and he didn't give a damn what one thought of the way he looked. He got up from the round bar table, taking his key ring with his sight dizzy and hands sweaty.

Using the table as his support, he tried to stand still and searched for his way out. A quick scan and he found a yellow flashing sign and the word 'Exit' blinking in red next to it. Collecting him together and leaving behind sleekly rolled bills of currency note to tip the server, he said goodbye to his buddies and walked towards the amber signboard.

Before leaving the tavern, he used the restroom, for he had mixed too many drinks for one night. Splashing the water on his face, he patted his cheeks and shook his head, but nothing made sense to him. The mirror he stared into was wall-mounted, encircled by a frame of threadlike strands of copper, and it was spinning anti-clock halfway, then returning to its origin; he watched the movement.

"Renil! Come on," He called his name, slapping himself hard and then went for the upper pocket of his shirt. Finding the third, the final stash and poured the white powder with his muggy hands onto the creased paper. He tore a piece of paper from the poster on the wall by the basin. Snorting the asymmetrical line on the paper, he kept his eyes closed until his nostrils went ice cold. His body absorbed the substance within moments. Staring back in the mirror, he saw everything crystal clear. He ran his hands in his hair, adjusted his shirt and he moved out of the water closet after dumping the useless crumpled piece of paper in the trash.

The stream of neurotransmitters that control the integral chemicals in the brain got disrupted temporarily. His body temperature had shot up, and his eyes turned devilish by the time he stepped outside the tavern.

The street was located eleven blocks from the tavern, and he got to his location in less than an hour. The recent dose of cocaine was cracking through his senses, and he had hiked all the way to the park at the end of the road strip.

After about two miles of wandering, he had finally found what he was searching for, the house numbers were ascending and had reached eighty–three. He searched around repeating in his head for a number, *ninety*, going back and forth a couple of rounds. He finally stopped and tried to read the number on the plate in front of him, but before he could complete reading the streetlight short-circuited.

VII

Three men in lab coats were standing at the small pavement outside the big frame steel door behind the 'crime scene' barricade tape, an investigation department van stood outside on the road next to the park and a group of responding officers were moving in and around the house.

He always walked to the crime scene. In his mid-twenties, of medium height, broad-shouldered, robust, poised and phlegmatic – his face was stern, long-boned, with a pointed chin and clear-skinned. The sedan stopped a block from the house, dropping the sleuth. If you wanted competence, he was your man.

On approaching the footsteps of the porch, he unbuttoned his blazer and confirmed his identity, taking a card from its breast pocket, flashing it to the officer standing at the taping. Joel Angus – Consulting Detective. The guard moved his hat in acknowledgement and raised the barricading band to make way for the man.

He was a master at deduction. He just listened, read body language and followed the eye movements. A picture at an angle, furniture and objects misplaced, a footprint going the wrong way. He noticed things no one else did. Well versed with combat techniques including Jujutsu and Judo, he was competitive both mentally and physically. Highly useful with his consulting, he had helped with many investigations for the city of Radena. And this time he was doing a favour to a friend.

He made his way inside the house stepping through the yellow taping, scrutinizing it from the corner of his eyes.

He went directly to the upper floor and arrived at the victim's room. They had taken away the bodies, and an outline marked on the mattress explained their positions. He looked just for a minute at the chalked sketch and corn-silk wallpapered room. Private eyes were reading the ceilings, the windows and the walls, trying and re-imagining the manslaughter.

In a broad gaze, he turned and stepped past the brown king-sized bed, out through the sandy wooden door. He eyed something peculiar, and he moved back inside the room. Halfway inside and the much half on the outside blocking the doorway, he moved his upper body to change his angle of sight to the wall on his left-hand side. A circular formation on the wall camouflaged very well with the wallpaper of the room. Moving to the adjacent room, he asked the officer for the reporting logbook.

He pressed the root of his nose as to remind himself of the insignia he had seen lately. The memory palace technique helped him recall, it was John Adams School. The observations section on the log as if confirming his guess mentioned – the emblem of John Adams School.

He asked the log keeper standing next to him if they inquired at the victim's workplace. The officer commented they were waiting for the telephone line to open as it was too early to make contact.

"I'll check with you in some time," he said and left for the lower floor.

VIII

The voice on the other end replied, "John Adams High School, good morning!"

"Hello there," the officer continued in an indifferent tone and almost instantly gave the female phone attendant the information about her boss. Her tone fumbled right after the news broke out and repeated, "Mr Anthony… Mr Victor Anthony murdered!"

"Yes," that was the unsympathetic reply she received.

It took her a few moments to acknowledge that the phone line was still live, and the caller was waiting on her. Mr Anthony was not only her boss but a greatly respectable figure, he was the provost.

"I want you to answer some questions," the stern voice repeated to find out that the message was clear. The line went blank for a few minutes before she retrieved the call.

"This was helpful," the caller thanked her and dropped the line.

IX

Heat licked at his sunburnt face and coiled around his limbs like a great hot-blooded serpent. The ground smouldered and sent up a disorientating haze. Even the birds were silent and the dust stood still as if too hot to move. The scorched, intense white rays of sun drenched him in his sweat, the salty droplets dripping on the concrete floor.

The cylindrical structure with the dome above in ruins had trapped the sun and sheltered him all morning, but there was no more shade. The sun had grown stronger, as if in vengeance, and was overhead now. Rubbing his eyes, he opened them for a fuller view, but the eyelids kept flickering. He looked away from the sun and towards the chamber he was inside.

The patch on the ceiling allowed the beams of sunlight in straight lines to pass through and trouble the eyes. Raising one hand, using the shadow from it, he ditched the light and tried to look through.

The building surely looked old. It spread over the imperfect surface, blemishes and ruptures that only adds to the emptiness. The hexagon was dust-coated, and an auditorium dome was like a beach awash with sand-filled waves. The colour on the walls wore off, the room was without furnishings, and a single piece, piece of metal hung on the sidewall. A set of staircases designed counterclockwise to reach atop. This is all that he assumed it to be.

He tried to change his position but failed to hold himself. Irritability was uncontrollable, to add to the hunger and anxiety. His head ached, throbbing created a sensation of the ring, like a spot of light, and he felt pressure on the eyeball. Paranoia kept coming like flashbacks from the past night. As much as he tried to bear it, the pain came out like an uproar from his throat as a silent scream.

In a semi-sleep state, his eyes met with a pair of black helpless eyes. Focusing to see through them, they reflected his image, as if a looking glass. His blunt hands were steady as they lifted the gun. Trying a dry shot, eyes blood red with a nefarious grin on his face, he nodded to himself. He was ready, and before he could look beyond the trigger pulled automatically.

The sound of a gunshot in his head jolted his body and woke him fully. Flashback of a dream, he hesitantly conjectured. He tried to move again using his core muscles but could not succeed, instead, the gut muscle cramped, and he vomited. The saliva from the side of his mouth drooled and mixed with the dust on the floor. The slimy liquid was gooey, and the strong odour compelled him to shift.

Pushing from the hands, somehow, he picked up himself, crawling away from the liquid thrown freshly out from his oesophagus. He grabbed onto the columns, the only complete thing which had not crumbled by uncounted days of the time the establishment had withstood. Wiping his lips from the sleeves, he stroked his head and laboured mentally to recall but could not carry out his thoughts as the substance was still swimming inside of him.

The only thing he could conclude was that he was at a tower top.

X

The elegant dining table below a low watt florescent bulb held most of the space the darkroom offered, the tall chairs finished in chestnut colour came from the same tree as the table, it seemed, the wall painting along the stairs had five white horses drawn, the neutral beige carpet spread through the stairs mixed well along the white and gold painted quaint chandelier which hung before the upper floor, blending beautifully with the ambience.

He had broken into the house and had no memory of how he manoeuvred the key lock system. Making way through the stairs, as cautious as a cat planning to enter the room, he gave a gentle push with a fingertip on the door to his right. It yielded soundlessly.

The room was empty. He walked inside. It had a single bed, a bookshelf and a dark-coloured coffee table kept under the curtained window. Also, it had a wardrobe closet. He stretched his hand to open the wardrobe. It had two pillows and hanging clothing. He went for the clothing, a grey hoodie. It had stitching on the back in the shape of a shield with two lions facing one another. The logo reads, 'To be, rather than to seem'.

It was a slogan he knew by heart.

From the opened closet he took one pillow and then left without making a sound. He put his fingers on the door, the second door on the right, the room that remained closed and gave it a similar but gentler push. But this time the hinges emitted a long and piercing squeak. The hinge felt as if someone endowed it with supernatural life and was barking like a watchdog to warn the sleepers of the house. The door had given the alarm. It seemed impossible that the dreadful din would not arouse the household as effectively as an earthquake. He stayed where he was. Several minutes passed, but nothing stirred.

He dared to peer into the room. The lights were dim; a knee-length side table by the bed had a pair of reading glasses with a neck string and a photo frame behind the plain water jug. The refraction through the jug showcased a picture of a middle-aged man with his wife and his son by his shoulders, the floral clothing with shorts, all three standing by the beach. A perfect family picture inflamed his vexation.

A brown coloured full-size bed with a long headrest and a robe hanging by the side of it was the resting place of a man, his wife hugging him from behind, drowsing.

Making his way inside the room delicately he loosened his shirt from behind his back, allowing the weapon to breathe and arranged the pillow in its position, quietly placing it on the shoulder of the man.

It woke him.

Recovering from his sleep, the man searched for his glasses, tapping softly on the side table. Helpless black eyes met the assailant. Killers never wait. Trigger pulled, and the bullet made its way from the barrel through the pillow, piercing the heart of its victim. All this happened in less time than it takes to tell. Blood was the only thing that could escape through the moment. The pillow instantly tattered to pieces, and the cotton had turned red, it sprinkled all around the room like snowflakes.

The woman screamed, waking up fitfully. He pointed the weapon at her.

XI

The beginning is always fun, filled with lying, cheating and stealing. He cared for nothing else but money, quickly made profits and a lot of affluent friends who shopped from him only and stayed until the drug stash lasted. He bought knives to cut his birthday cakes and a pistol for his promotion. The hunger grew, being crazy, loopy, sounds amusing from the outside, not so much from the inside. Everything he held dear fell by the wayside. Misery comes at the end.

He had many signs of abuse, had become withdrawn, his personality sunk in dark thoughts and his athletic frame weakened. Money disappearing from purses and items of value had slowly vanished. 'I was always in control,' he thought so, but drugs had gripped, and he did not realize when and how he no longer had control.

The body pain was as real as gravity, and it brought him back to his present. Standing with the support of the wall holding onto one column, he regretted taking the white powder drug, the cocaine. Memories of the past hovered his thoughts, he felt responsible for the miseries of his mother and his father's loss in the stock game, cursing why he was born.

The dark emotions are like salt, just a pinch adds flavour, yet too much of it ruins the entire dish. One must remember what food is and what is salt. Love, integrity, self-belief and confidence – that's food; guilt, hate, anger and sloth are the salt. He had vastly more salt than food. The awful hollowness, the waves of wretchedness threatened to engulf his mind. He leaned against the column in despair, screamed louder in pain, pulled his hair, cried and fell on his buttock sitting on the floor.

Slowly he shook his head in denial, but the reality weighed too heavy for the conscience, the weight of negativity was burying him alive. He lifted his head, trying to come out of it and into the blankness of the space. The rays of the late afternoon fell slanting through the blemished dome directly on a small metal object. It looked like a hilt of a sword, with a smaller lever that produced a loud bang when pressed.

He hastily reached for the pistol. The weapon was simply to push people away and to stay in the drug game. His heart fell silent to an empty chamber. It spared no bullets. The 9mm had a slot for seven, but he owned only three bullets. The past day passed like thousands of camera frames per second shown one at a time. In this slow time bubble, it warbled everything. Mr Anthony's long, newly wrinkled face was clear as crystal. He could see himself in the eyes of the old man, but it was too late. Not only the provost of John Adams but an innocent lady who was sleeping peacefully with her husband got punished. His hands shook, followed by his body, and finally, it shook his soul. The memory induced an unbearable pain for not only the head but for the heart. He wailed.

Life is a unique gift given by God for us to learn, love and be patient. The words of his mother echoed in his head. But he gave his gift to the devil, chose abhorrence and vexation. To give help and support to one another is the most humanly attribute, she had always told him, but he was a savage, murdering an innocent couple.

He kicked and pushed the weapon away. Moments later, he reached for it again. The two missing bullets found the fatality in Victor Anthony and his wife. He suddenly went white as chalk. His eyes and mouth were frozen wide open in stunned surprise. He impulsively checked his pockets, but the pockets were empty. He checked again but found nothing.

'What about the third bullet?'

XII

A mutter of thunder winds growling, ominous dark clouds gathering and a sudden downpour, again.

Turning the light-coloured file upside down, he pushed it towards the tall man sitting comfortably in his chair across the table. Stroking the pen on the paper, he signed and closed the Manila file and kept it on the pile lying at his home office table. Looking at his watch, an hour and a half of discussion he suggested, "Shall we?"

"Sure," the person across the table replied.

The man working from home was Inspector Kadin. He stood up to shake hands with the sleuth. Joel told his goodbye, and the inspector moved away from the chair and started walking with him towards the outside of his office room.

"Finally, the case is closed," the officer exclaimed, admiring the wits of the man walking next to him.

"After weeks of intelligence from field officers and police department, we made it possible," Joel replied.

"But we paid the price of three innocent lives," he added.

"You are a modest man," the chief patting the back continued, "and I am confident this microchip tracking is an efficient technique."

Through a chip pinned on the psychopath criminal named Haiden, the investigation had concluded, and the killer got caught. The consultant detective had arranged and tagged the chip on the psycho.

They walked in silent agreement through the living room.

Standing at the feet of the building, the car waited for the sleuth, but before they could exchange the pleasantries for the night, the doorbell rang. A tall, lean man was standing across the door. He must be in his forties, yet he had a build of a teenager. He greeted both the men by taking off his hat and placing it under his armpit.

"It's never good when a patrol officer comes to you later in the evening," Joel asserted.

The inspector opened the door and introduced him to the tec. He is one of our most diligent patrolmen. Adiel offered his salute, and Joel replied by exchanging a smile and extending his hand. He shook the hand in contentment, and the dampness of the hand of the police officer was easily noticeable. Then he asked the Inspector for privacy because of the protocol.

"Adiel, go on, it's completely fine," Inspector said.

Patrol officer Adiel had been driving back to the police station post-lunch the same afternoon when he saw a clique of seven young men on the sidewalk. It seemed from a distance the group of sports enthusiasts discussing a recent win of their football fan club. Pulling the pedal off the gas, he dropped the pace of the patrol car to neutral and soon what seemed to be a discussion about sports came to be a process of exchange, of something of palm-sized wrapped inside a transparent pouch.

To affirm the guess, he waited. The men suspiciously looked on either side of the road and carefully exchanged the salt like substance in a shake of hands. The men were dealing drugs. Pushing the gas pedal, Adiel rushed towards the group, not giving away the siren. The men quickly spread in smaller groups, noticing the patrol car making a turn in their direction.

The car chased the two men who had exchanged the cocaine on the sidewalk. Speeding up the vehicle, the patrolman quickly reached towards the corner of the road no. 47.

Following the two men, he applied the hand brakes simultaneously turning the handle close to the stomach and in a blink of the eye the silver patrol car drifted through the footpath bumping through the sidewalk back on the roadway, barely missing the glass entrance of the flower shop in the front.

Completing the short distance of the road and sliding leftward, he reached the gas station oblique. Suddenly a stone came pelting without warning from the driving side of the car. He crouched, and rounds of pelting followed. The window glass that was protecting the cop from sideways shattered instantaneously and the car wobbled fitfully.

While maintaining the same body position, he signalled on the microphone for help, "I am near shell gas station, road no. 47, hurry up!"

Receiving a positive response from the other end, "Gas station, road no. 47, copy that," he released his grip from the shoulder transmitter. He knew it would take a couple of minutes before help would arrive, but the gang he was messing with, they were in no mood to wait. Devastating the patrol vehicle, they made it impossible for him to get out.

Three men continued dashing and then cut off, leaving behind a terror of deep silence. Officer waited and tried listening to background noises, but nothing seemed to make any sound. He raised his head slowly to where he could see through the diamond-shaped logo on the steering wheel of his Renault Megane and observe what was going around.

It was still hazy and quiet.

Visibility enhanced slowly and he could see the stretch, the main driveway, with few parked cars on both sides of the pavement as usual. At the far end, a heavy-duty vehicle was standing diagonally, blocking the access road.

The young lads were jumping frantically from the driving side of the two-wheelers and running towards the opposite direction of the blocked road. The two men he had been following were the last to leave his sight, escaping from the far end disappeared behind the shell gas station.

Moving out of the car as quickly as possible, he began running towards the truck. He paced as fast as he could with all his strength, but before he could cover the distance, the truck exploded in bright daylight.

Inspector Kadin pursed his lips and exclaimed, "Thank God, it rained today."

Adiel spoke again, "I have already given my statement at the police station and there were no casualties, but I wanted to be sure that I report it personally to you, Sir."

"And I found this near the front wheel," he continued. Pulling out the bindle paper, he lifted it to his shoulder height.

Both the men to whom he had narrated the incident observed the bindle paper – a small metal ring with a short chain and a small decoration. They looked at it for a moment.

Inspector Kadin saw a marking on it.

After a long pause, he broke the silence, "Call for the office clerk and ask him to find me the results that match."

XIII

The wind pushed on the car to no avail. They were going forward and nothing but a blessed tragedy can change that. The tires made their monotonous hiss over the rain-washed highway. The road was straight. It took seconds for the eye to travel its length into the blue-grey horizon in the far distance. They had driven the car through the city into the highway, leaving behind the hustle-bustle and the noise.

Not much of a road trip as the destination was close by. An old structure on the opposite side held Joel's attention.

The chauffeur proactively mentioned, "A prayer hall."

The road was empty of traffic; the day was sunny, but the clouds that were drawn partially made it look grey. It had been just a few minutes since they passed the minaret and then the car derailed from the smooth roadway into a narrow path, probably farmland.

What Adiel found near the truck wheel was a small article manufactured by G&M. They contacted the company, and they gave them the address information after an extensive search through their record.

The chauffeur and the passenger wobbled inside the car while the vehicle was keeping up with the gravel road beneath. Dust kept chasing the trail of the car and they advanced in steep terrain. The stones skipping up were hitting the car's body while the one lane wide road turned round.

Moments later a small pond came into the view. Applying the handbrakes, the chauffeur halted the sedan and asked hesitatingly, "Should we advance further?"

Joel signalled the driver to wait and moved out of the vehicle. He inspected the view and the cabin that stood beyond against the sunny yet cloud-covered sky. All he could see was the crumbling walls that were nothing more than a ghostly silhouette of some previous existence.

It was a house that had you hesitant to even step through the doorway.

Taking his hands out from his pockets, he stepped away from the car. Reaching for the vest pocket of his suit, he adjusted the concealed-hammer locked revolver hanging comfortably in its holster.

Walking away from the car he moved towards the short narrow trail beside the pond and soon the trees and the large stones of the topography absorbed him.

The abandoned house stood composedly as if it had chosen solitude for itself, a cabin surrounded by wild plantation and weed and the house board kissing the ground. It was an accommodation offered as a charity rather than a choice.

Walking through the uncultured grass, he reached the structure which stood in front. It was old and rusty, and with every approaching step it seemed to deteriorate a little more than before. Smudged walls were of the auburn orange which must have had been the original wall paint. The wooden flooring had a hollow patch in front of the entrance door. The handrail on one side was missing completely, and a rocking chair was dumped across the foot of the side window.

Coldwater seeps through window frames, rotten and blistered, to nurse the mildew and raise wallpapers that peel. Fragments of plaster lie damp over the floor on the entrance, their only purpose to soak in the seasonal rain.

The damaged stair entrance had the main door partially open, clearly, no one had repaired it for a very long time. The doors hang from the side as if slammed hard, often, and the scuff marks, chips and scratches became visible as he came near. He stepped on the broken stairs leading to the home and made his way gently through the door. He could sense it, the disaster, but it was worse than he had imagined.

XIV

Grey matter which dominates the memories was pumping back to the brain along with the other important mental chemicals, but the clutches of hallucinogen still prevailed.

It was the darker stage of twilight, the time for shadows to get long and hard. He walked past the lawn towards the broken patch in front of the doorstep when his eyes met his father's. The old man was drunk and swinging in intoxication, he had his hands gripped around his woman's neck, cursing her.

A thwack followed to the milk-white face of his mother.

Renil had swallowed the anger when it was fire-seed and forgot to drink something cool, so it grew in his belly until it came out like lava from a volcano. He ran towards his father and jumped on the old man, instantaneously, putting him to the ground. The rage made him throw a punch, but the only difference was he felt no pain.

With no intention to stop, he kept exerting his energy until the old man's face got bloody. Rokaya tried her best to separate the two but possessed with anger, rage and revenge he kept pushing her away. His mother grabbed him from his back and pulled him hard to disjoin. He was a mad dog, but she tamed him temporarily.

He got up on his feet while his father remained lifeless on the floor. He ran around the house and came back as quickly as he had gone. His shirt was tucked out when he returned. Taking out the top-break revolver from the back of his jeans, he aimed it at the man lying on the ground.

Staring at the weapon, her jaw dropped in disbelief.

She recognized him as her boy. His eyes of pure mischief and a heart of gold.He had that way of moving that honest people do with the spark of the child and a smile that went all the way through to his core. He was surely not the boy she had raised. The haughty look reflected on his face gave her shudders. His hands were tightly closed around the icy surface of the metallic grey coloured revolver. He seemed to have no sense of humanity. His heart had turned stone cold.

She pleaded with him to stop the madness and asked him to leave the weapon. He didn't move, eyes were devil red and his father's blood was dripping off his face. She appealed again. The words were barely falling on his ears. He could not hear her, could see her begging for mercy, but felt nothing.

'This has to happen,' he told himself.

Helpless, she tried to snatch the gun from her son. He retaliated and tried to push her away. The two mingled for a moment, and suddenly the gunshot echoed as if it had cracked a skull. The noise reverberated in the ears and rang out far over the boundaries of the house.

His limbs flex in shock, and his eyes open to the sound. Looking around relieved him, he was still under the hexagonal dome and it was yet another dream. The sweat was drizzling from his temples down his face, his body felt heavy and with much effort, he raised his arm to wipe off the dampness of the face. He felt pain, a little on the forehead but more on the back of his hand, at his fingers, the knuckles. They were all swollen and red.

His bowels churned suddenly as it reminded him of the third bullet which went missing from the revolving slot.

XV

The door fully opened to two adult bodies lying on both sides of the room, and the floor turned into a dried pool of blood. The first room after climbing the broken stairs of the entrance had tobacco pungency. He found nothing except for a ruffle of clothes, buds of cigarettes and some empty bottles of whisky.

Making his way to the smaller room which only had a bed and a utility trunk in it was neat compared to the room he had visited before. The walls were patchy and punctured with the marks of a struggle, fist marks. He searched the place quickly but found nothing significant. Moving around the kitchen cum storeroom he observed the walls were unwashed, and the counter coated with years of dust. But nothing seems to be out of the place.

Coming back to the area where the bodies lay like ghoulish mannequins, he waited to read them. The body that was lying on the floor was of a male. A tattered mess of old clothes and muck. He seemed to be someone who busied himself with drinking, mostly with beer or a glass of whisky and chips in easy reach. He was grave and expressionless; sort of parent that never speaks much to their children didn't build those go-carts or dance with them on songs, not the kind of parents children enjoy their time with.

His gaze shifted and found something around the passage between the television room and the entrance door. Slowly reaching he picked it using his disposable gloves, he observed the small piece which was half broken. A marble cut statue of a man sitting on his knees, his palms facing inward in the posture of prayer.

Before leaving the house to its fate, he looked at the lady sitting with a bullet mark in the centre of her neck, despite the desiccated blood around the shoulder blades in straight lines she wore a look of serenity, hope, beatitude, a little short of radiance. She was someone who must be always praying, her lips mumbling the verses, she had soft light brown eyes, the exact shade of latte, a ring of gold hung inside her iris, adding another layer of depth to her already beautiful eyes, despite being dead, her hair black, tied inside the doughnut bun, face as white as milk with a tint of cherry on the cheeks and scars all over. She seemed to be a believer.

Leaving the marble cut souvenir back where it was, he left the cabin.

XVI

The fields were all around, through the tinted windows. Gazing straight ahead, the world outside continued like some choreographed dance, but without the soul, it should have.

Psychiatry, time devoted to observing animal behaviour, astrology, studies of the stars and the mediation lessons were his prime sources of deduction and intelligence. Everything he was he learnt during his time with his wildling master.

His phone rang. It was his old friend.

Joel replied, "I'll do it for you."

Before the call interrupted his thoughts, he had been staring at tiny cashew shaped equipment. It had a hook on the tip of it resembling a microphone like ones used for television, theatre and public speaking applications to allow for hands-free operation.

The sedan was running fast and looking through the glass window, he tried to work on the case, basis the officer's log they timed the death of the husband-wife to midnight hours. The truck explosion occurred in the daytime and the most recent killings, the third part of the puzzle, presumably occurred at the crack of dawn considering the odour of the bodies and the dehydrated blood.

But there was no lead to follow except for the name of the suspect.

Repeating and going through the series of incidents, he kept his mind engaged with the possibilities.

Troubled youth are not the concern, they have experienced trouble, and they are communicating their desperate need however they can that they need to escape their trouble. They long for acceptance and need forgiveness. And they can have it only from someone who has the divinity to extend it.

The marble cut statue of a man sitting on his knees, his palms facing inward in the posture of prayer, crossed his mind.

He asked himself, 'Who would pardon the troubled youth'

It bolted him. Shifting in his seat, he leaned forward and asked the driver to change their direction. The chauffeur pulled the column down and the right indicator blinked, turning the three-pronged star logo at the bonnet in the told direction. The car went pacing on the highway in the opposite direction.

Waiting patiently in his seat, he checked his timepiece. It was a quarter to five. Convinced he will find his subject soon. He adjusted his blazer sleeve for crispness.

The destination was closer than it seemed. Fiddling with the rear mirror, the chauffeur checked, "Where to, Sir?"

"There is no sin, no crime, no evil that God cannot forgive," he replied sitting comfortably in the back seat hoping that the delay mustn't cost another life.

XVII

The encephalon had patchy responses from the sensory receptors. The motor reception travelling from spine to cerebrum was weak and moratorium. Low consciousness and excruciating pain had hampered his decision making. The mental turbulence took a toll on his senses.

He felt the emptiness in his heart, barren as the moor on a desolate winter morn, a shear of nothingness that somehow takes over and holds the soul and threatens to kill one entirely. The weight of the world was resting on his shoulders and there is nothing he can do to get out from under it.

An emotional predicament, the death of his mother left an unbearable pain in his heart. It soiled his soul. The only person who truly loved him cared for him, never hated him. She was dead, and he had put her to the grave. Her memories plagued him with shame and negativity. He was in the court of self-judgement, his past was the witness, his present guilty. He was trying his case, and the punishment must be of the highest conduct.

His deeds had demolished all the reasons for him to live. He had climbed the staircase unconsciously and was going up on the ledge, in the attempt to set himself free from all his vices. It would wipe all the malice, the past would be a clean slate, and the suffering would end.

This was his nirvana.

He looked down from the height for one last time. The iron clad gateway was rustic, and designed bars stood on gates in straight lines, their top spear-like pointed and protected. The driveway road is covered with stabilized soil. A park stood facing the tower, equally primitive, and the dusted walls around the minaret were presumably its square border. He suspended his arms in the air and closed his bleary eyes in his last moments.

The cool breeze touched his face. His thumping heart pacing at every beat. Distance between suffering and liberation was marginal – the pavement. He was standing on the decisive step, one step forward and no return.

The sound of the gong brought erection of hairs on his skin.

"Time for the evening prayer," the words echoed in his head, fresh as if the first time and brought flashback of his first visit – holding his mother's hand, walking through the driveway admiring the park and the big building. The tower was a prayer hall, he recalled.

The Gods were his witness, an arrangement made for the trial, and he had accepted and confessed to the sins.

Despite a suicidal mission, he was hopeful, and the salty tears of contentment flowed unchecked down his cheeks.

'I am sorry, Ma.'

Part Two

XVIII

The tower grew from the ground as an albino plant reaching for the sun. They built it in good times, in days of peace. One could tell that from the generously sized doors and windows.

Its former owner had abandoned the 57m tall and adequately wide standing structure under the false impressions of being haunted. A missionary, St. Ajabel renovated and changed the building into a prayer hall.

Arriving at the entrance, Joel left the car and sprinted inside. Hustling through the entrance of the crowded tower, he made to the back door before they sealed it. Backdoors always save time and allow bypassing of the security check.

The art and architecture of the minaret were influential despite injuries to the spiral tower from the past decades, the stucco carvings represented floral and geometrical designs. Walls panelled with mosaics of dark blue glass, the interior was spacious and had nine aisles in the praying area.

Looking for access to reach the top of the tower he scanned the entire hall hurriedly, but the clump of aficionados centred towards the stage was all he could see. Ecstasy was in full swing and everybody was moving in unison of one colour, that of celebration. A few zealots standing at the foot of the staircase worked as his cue to identify where the stairs started from and reaching them quickly, he climbed them. With quick steps, he covered the length of the tower and reached the crest.

The door of the roof was open, the dome above looked ocean blue, and one could see the clear evening sky from its blotch. The ledge was partially visible, and the counter clock spiral stairs on his left-hand side would provide a fuller view.

He looked around and found the bisque-coloured walls with a good deal of rhombus-shaped openings from the bottom stretched to the top of the hexagonal dome.

A weapon was lying unattended on the floor, a pistol. He quickly checked the magazine, and it was empty. Leaving it as is, he ascended the stairs as fast as he could.

The boy was on the pavement.

Words softly travelled to the eardrums of the figure standing on the edge, on the ultimate step.

Renil wasn't sure what was happening – was this his subconscious mind doing the final talking?

His senses demanded a conclusion, and it made him halt the mission of self-killing.

"God, help those who help themselves," the magical voice came closer.

"You cannot decide the time of your departure."

"It's prayer time, please step down," the source of the sound demanded.

The words reminded him of his mother and instantly his arms came back to his sides. The comforting words created a dilemma, "Is it you, Ma?"

Before he could confirm, he was back on the ground and away from the ledge.

"People may leave you but God never will," the benign voice replied.

If God brings you to it, he will bring you through it.

Trust the timings, Renil. It was a male voice.

The sound of his name washed his face blank with surprise like his brain cogs couldn't turn fast enough to take the information.

His face registered with shock.

Dusk came sooner than expected. Looking away from the horizon he turned and opened his eyes slowly and found a man of equal height, robust, in a crisp suit smiling back at him.

"Time's up," he declared.

A Christmas present in the bindle paper was his evidence.

XIX

The tower welcomed a greater audience and a complete celebration on its Founder's Day. Despite being on the highway, it attracted people from the nearby zones to be part of the ceremony.

The run-away boy got frisked before leaving the rooftop. The back door was a simple and efficient plan for exit.

They had to wait for the prayer to end for the guild of devotees to settle. He checked the antediluvian wall clock and waited. The devotees were queuing for the blessing from the man at the podium on the centre stage.

The flooded aisles could not hold the crowd, and it got diverted to the centre stage. The back door would be the safest option, thus the two were standing near the stairway.

A crowd formed faster than thought and had covered the entire hall, including the back door and stairway in less than a few minutes. He pushed the boy and signalled him to move away from the crowd, taking a step back. The boy obeyed, and he moved but not in the direction asked.

Joel suspected what he was up to and quickly tightened his grip.

In the transition of stepping back, he tugged and jumped into the thicket and instantly became part of the crowd. He was like a leaf floating in the wind, like sails without a boat, carefree and joyful, and his seeker stared like the helpless tree with tangled roots.

He got pushed far ahead of the stairway from where he started. Joel tried his best to keep up with the swarm, he pushed hard but the task at hand was next to impossible. The chants grew louder along with the sound of the gong hanging from the tower top which echoed throughout the hall, adding to the difficulty to concentrate. They waived the holy flags from the centre stage clogging the horde putting everyone to look upward in amazement and hysteria. Bulldozing his way forward, somehow, he got through the centre. He twisted around to a tap on the shoulder and saw the ecclesiastic waiting on him to collect the ceremonial sweets.

"Who is the in-charge of this gathering?" The sleuth demanded.

The chaplain looked confused. He flashed his sophisticated revolver from the inner pocket of his suit and pressed the question again, loudly.

The holy man answered after he sneaked through the compact weapon resting inside the vest holster.

"His name is Amram."

Everyone around the aisles was tossing and turning, eager to shake hands with the priest, and so was he eager to get out of the mess. Joel had entered the tower in pursuit of his subject, but there it placed him amidst the multitude going berserk for the offerings and touch of the holy man.

He gave away the offering as quickly as he received it to the woman next to him and hurried back on his mission, crossing the whirlpool of homo sapiens.

Arriving at the corner of the stage, he realized he was still too far to pursue his prey, and the boy was swiftly transported to the main door exit by the congregation.

Running away, the boy turned, and at that moment locked eyes with his pursuer. In your eyes is your humanity; the person you are. The eyes that stared back at him were of a hunter framed in the passionless face of an executioner, the look pierced through his soul.

Time slowed for Joel, as if his brain needed a photograph, a keepsake to give him reason in the time to come. Then, after time unmeasurable, the gong bell rang, bringing him back into his moment, as if this gong was the clock, the only timekeeper that mattered.

The boy disappeared in front of his eyes with one mighty leap.

Keeping his calm, he pulled out his cellular device from his pocket.

The voice mentioned loud and clear, "Go to the main gates and bar them with whatever you can find. Tell them Amram gave such orders."

Before the voice on the other side could affirm, the phone disconnected.

The chauffer instantaneously made his way outside the vehicle and hasted towards the iron clad gateway to carry out the orders.

XX

A luxury white coloured sedan with a circular designed logo stating letters BMW stood affront, manned by two.

The man standing next to the boot was tall, dark-skinned and well built. His face heavy and moustache trimmed, he wore a camel-coloured half-shirt, standing hard as a rock, with his arms crossed under his broad chest guarding the vehicle.

The front guard maybe was the driver, only visible to the head. He was as huge as the other man, and the guards were taking care of someone extra-special.

Rushing towards the parking, he planned to escape the place by running away, but now he felt intrigued by these men.

Working in the streets was not a choice but an alternative to avoid his father and his home. The guidance, parenting or his circumstances were never pleasing, but he was an intelligent boy because he knew what he feared, and he embraced it.

The sole reason he listened to the man in suit up on the tower roof was because of fear of death.

Trouble got to him unexpectedly, but he was still a kid at heart. Even an adult could not handle such an impulse of suicide. It was the right thing to do for him at that moment, but a fear caught him when he thought about the fall, thought about hitting the ground from such a height. He got rooted to the spot when the gong rang, frozen, heart in his mouth, incapacitated by fear.

He had already edged backwards before he heard the benign voice. It was a last-minute save for him.

From the moment he went down that ledge, he had been planning his escape.

Keeping his eyes and ears wide open, he skimmed his surroundings, which now comprised the parking, main entrance of the tower and the back door.

A deadly idea walloped.

Open, make space and close.

XXI

He checked his mobile phone; it had no notifications.

Making a way out through the steeple, the sight eased him, the gates next to the greensward, the entry gates to the tower, barricaded.

Brisk walking to the pylon, he found a few men talking to his chauffeur. With authority, he questioned the batch, "Anybody left after I called?"

"No chance, Sir," the chauffeur replied immediately.

"I reached the gates as soon as I got your instructions," he continued.

He looked around, putting his hands on his waist, observing everything in a glance. The gravel was empty, and the car queue was on the sidewall. The Park only had pigeons hopping and flitting. Looking back at the tower, he glimpsed at the top.

The gates being closed had slowly attracted many inquisitive figures, and people approached the means of access and egress.

"We need to check every vehicle that progresses through. A juvenile convict is trying to escape from this establishment," Joel ordered the men standing in front of him.

Amram was amongst the seven men included in the briefing.

Everyone nodded to the commands in agreement.

A skinny boy with a fair complexion, brown eyes, black hair, wearing a ragged white shirt and blue jeans is the one who we need to look for, spread the word let everyone work as a team.

Amram followed, walking up to the first car in the queue he looked at the man in the driving seat and requested politely, “Brother, we need to check your car.”

“Sure,” the man quickly opened the side door and stepped out.

“Please open the boot as well,” Amram added. It gave the intended message to the vehicle behind and the others following.

The impuissant boy was hiding in the darkness resembling his home. He was comfortably numb, curled up somewhere inside a compact space of the boot of a car, parked in the square walls of the complex.

He was watching the blackness, his heart hammering. No one can know about what had happened, not about his part in it. To them, it's a suspected carnage, but he had no gang affiliation. It's hard to get away from destiny. Fate favours the brave, but he's still a kid, a teenager but a child and whatever the fate of such kids, it isn't good.

He heard something which broke his numbness. There was a sound of the opening of the door, of the car he was in. He panicked and quickly made his way outside.

The hunt had begun.

XXII

The only occasion throughout the year when the holy place received some attention was today May 10th, the Founder's Day. Mostly the caretaker enjoyed his days at his home and seldom visited the abandoned space.

It was open to all, but it did not offer any prayer service, hence only a few people from nearby visited occasionally.

There was no one much interested in the repair work funding, and it had been last four years since the ceremony came into play as this minaret was the last-mentioned abode by the great savant St. Ajabel of Radena.

During his journey around the country, this was his ultimate destination before he parted from the materialistic world. The mention of the tower by one of the city's newspapers helped gain attendance on the foundation day each year.

The place had offered shelter to the savant and converted to the ceremonial ground only for one day, whereas on the other days it just acts as an ordinary building on the highway.

Organizers sent a request to the prayer priest to stay in his chamber until the traffic outside was smooth.

He never asked for the reason and nodded in agreement, waiting meekly.

Because the building was ancient, the chambers despite being huge were not very comfortable, but the aged man had no complaints. Pulling out his rosary from the robe, his fingers moved in the God's praise while sitting on the long wooden bench which lay right in the front.

He had very well-known beforehand about the time it can consume before he could depart. The sleuth's identification via federal weapon displayed on the stage was clear to comprehend the scenario.

He continued to pray.

XXIII

Renil stood still like a statue after jumping out silently, his back leaning against the trunk of the cherry red vehicle. Elevating his body by getting on his toes he tried to sneak, craning his neck, making his vision parallel to the rear windshield he verified the road, the park and the tower.

A mass breakdown of cars, everyone in his sight was checking their cars with opened boots.

Looking at the situation, the tables have turned and the escape using a vehicle was impossible. Crawling his way, he made it to the SUV, which was standing in proximity to the white sedan, the only car parked in the lane next to his. The men still guarding the sedan, a luxury car he could only dream of.

Looking around, he found the way to the main door of the tower to be clear of people. Everyone was outside the prayer hall by then. Now, he had to choose between the abandoned tower and the guarded white automobile. Either he can try his chance with the giants, or he could avoid all the fiasco and go back to the roof tower and stay low key until the scrutiny is over and walk out later when the darkness falls, similar to the way he might have arrived in.

With temptation and bewilderment, he advanced, knowing it could be the moment of truth for him and his seeker.

Joel realised why the young man agreed to step down from the ledge and then he organized against Renil by ordering a vehicle inspection.

Completing a quick brief about ensuring a survey of each vehicle, he left to check the insides of the tower. The men nodded in understanding, and he went back inside the establishment.

He knew where to start from, the tower roof. One of the least suspected places topped the checklist. To outsmart him wasn't so easy.

The prayer hall was almost empty, and aware of the ingress and the brim, he climbed his way to the roof comfortably. The door was still open and gave a similar yet suspicious look. The pursuer could sense someone on the top. He cautiously moved towards it from the railing.

XXIV

Categorically this for the first time, the run-away boy prayed for a miracle to happen.

The door opened from the left comfortably. He observed the man who was approaching him. The boy riffled through his surrounding to confirm he was incognito. By the time he focused back, the man was at the top of the stairs. He shut his eyes and waited a little longer, enjoying his last breath of freedom. What he wished for was impossible, he secretly knew.

Time to face reality and take things the way they are.

The man was descending the stairs, and he didn't move. He stood there in wonder, eyes popping out. The man stopped and searched the staircase again, and the last ray of hope dwindled.

Renil covered his mouth and nose, cancelling the noise of respiration.

He waited.

The man surveyed again. What he thought, adieu to the past, was a reinstatement.

He wondered why people prayed, why they yielded physical and material pleasures, why did they devote so much time of their life, why offer devotion, when the only thing given in return was misery. What was the significance of the structure which stood as a holy abode? What was the relevance to putting your trust in Gods?

And what happened next was unbelievable!

They left the car alone. The guards ran towards the man descending the stairs in his white robe. Renil could not believe his eyes. Near about the final few steps of the stairs, the elderly man had fumbled his footing. He had not fallen but was misbalanced and both the men ran to offer him support and establish confirmation of well-being.

His faith restored, his lucky star shining bright, and adieu indeed. His moment to seize, he followed as planned – open, make space and close. Placing him comfortably inside the spacious trunk of the sedan, he thought about the man in the suit who had sniffed him and was still in hot pursuit.

Joel looked down from the tower and saw the white automobile pacing through the gravel road, the only vehicle which got past without the check.

A sudden sunrise beats the owl.

XXV

The weights lifted from his shoulders as if an overly large child had just leapt off after a satisfying piggyback ride. He laughed at his wickedness, felt his skin to ensure it was real, and giggled again.

"Perhaps that's it," he concluded after a lengthy wait.

He was finally exiting the emotional storm. They could not track him any longer. The thought made him optimistic.

Hope was radiating in to soothe his blood he felt it right into his bones.

The comfort of the boot was four-folds better than the bed and spacious enough for a cosy nap. He even found a case of water bottles, quickly tore it open and instantly gulped down a mini bottle and rested inside the dark. Set in place for nearly two hours relaxing, doing nothing sounds exciting, but is tedium and painful.

He was cautious before tossing in the dark space. Relying on hearing ability for awareness, he focused and tried to imagine what was happening outside and waited. The car was still. He was sure, didn't feel the pace and no rotational sound of tyres, but he waited.

Waiting sounds easy but not with full bladder, cold, aching muscles and boredom. After a due course of time, he thought and then prepared to step out. He recently had witnessed a miracle, so there was no point wasting time to pray for another.

Gathering all his wits and courage to face what waits outside, and with equal nervousness and enthusiasm, he opened the boot softly. It clicked, and the automated panel moved upwards, illuminating the expanse with subtle sunlight of the fading Helios and thick clouds.

He promptly stepped out of the vehicle.

Striving to walk ordinarily through the beautiful mountain road, his heart was repulsive and doing the opposite. It raced at an immense pace, making him feel it skipped a beat. The first thing he saw was the blue hatchback parked five yards away in the parking space and the man in the driving seat of the shabby four-wheeler staring at him.

Renil paused for a moment and realizing that nobody knows him, he acted confidently.

Ignoring the grown-up and his hatchback, he moved away from the parking and towards the road across the parking space which offered a superior view of the landscape and a sense of assured independence.

He wanted to turn around and find out, but he controlled himself and kept marching in the forward direction. He walked in the unknown, away from the clergy, his guards, the sedan and the blue hatchback.

The fresh air of the mountains helps forget the hardships. Embraced by nature, after a not so long walk through the curvy road, it guided him into the wild and provided him with the leeway.

The surroundings, the essence of trees, the music of natural forces, nature, blue sky, freshness in the air, topography, greenery and solace was surreal. The aura of the jungle, of a million wild souls, is as tangible as water when one bathes. It is another sense, one that comes to the heart rather than the eyes, as soaked in richness as they are. The combined natural forces charmed him.

He twirled around in his moment of liberation, ran, following his heart, then stopped to catch his breath and ran again. The joy was absolute, the crumbling of leaves beneath his feet, rays of the setting radium up above, the height of surrounding cedar trees, exactly like the stories his mother had told him.

He rejoiced the moment by lying comfortably on the ground with straightened feet and hands behind his neck.

He thought, 'In life, nothing happens at all or it all happens at once.'

With no warning, adulthood had knocked on his door. Life was his mentor, and the teaching had begun. Destiny had transported him to a land far from where he belonged.

'Do I belong anywhere?' He self-questioned.

He shrugged and reposed.

'What better place there could be to start afresh,' he laughed out loud.

XXVI

The nautical dusk is a phenomenon right before the darkness falls, the top of the sun gets around 12 degrees below the horizon and the night takes over. He continued through the beauty of nautical dusk, which had transfigured into trepidation of the night.

An alluring location was turning into treacherous land.

The night was plummeting, happiness had been a short-lived experience for the fledgling, and the dusk compelled him to embark on his expedition, an arduous undertaking in search of space to rest and sleep.

The walk was not as obvious to his experience. It caught his breath. Thinking about the worst, his thoughts wavered on getting lost, starvation or maybe getting killed by a predator. With no other option, he pushed himself a little further.

He trudged unresolved into the woodland looking for an elevated space, a cave or an abandoned camp, but the task was increasingly onerous. Because of the surreal ambience, he couldn't believe that he wouldn't encounter a pack of trolls or monsters on the go.

He paused again.

The freedom became taxing and footslogging through the woods was the reason for awful light-headedness. Also, absentia of nutrients fabricated his blood sugar. Before he could move any further, he collapsed, falling on his knees.

He grinned at his miseries, out from the frying pan and straight into the fire.

Looking around for a sense of direction, he was inside the living version of the stories he was told about when he was younger. There was no trace of civilization in this wilderness apart from a worn-out path that snaked through the blanket of grass. Around it, the vegetation was lush. As he tilted his head up, he saw the path fade into a void of mist and bare twigs.

The forest seemed like a glorious realm of the Gods guarded by demigods, but he was no hero and Gods have already played their part.

He had no food, no ally and no direction to follow.

XXVII

The right hand softly touched the poniard around the waist.

The elk calf was enjoying his last morsels before the night. Raptor waited patiently. The young wapiti raised his head to reassure if any danger surrounded him and after a subtle gap continued scooping the moss and the sapling. Out from its case, the poniard slashed the air and with great intensity made way through the skin of the animal. He jumped in reflex and pain, but it was worthless as the supple muscles of the neck got ruptured.

The predator walked out casually and introduced herself to the dangling elk.

Trying its best to run the poor thing could not move properly because the razor-sharp metal had pierced the windpipe of the prey. She strolled her way to her hunt and with folded hands thanked the elk for giving his life for her survival. She patted the forehead of the dying animal, and before it could close his eyes for the last time, the dagger twisted, taking his last breath away.

Cleaning the sharp tool with her cape she placed it back in its case and getting down on her knees tied the fore and the hind legs of her dinner efficiently and carried the calf on her shoulder to march on her way.

With speedy steps, she covered the distance and was reaching for her home when she found a frail structure at the trail before the hike to the chieftain.

It was a human body, a boy. He was unconscious, lifeless and lying on his stomach near the trail of shrubs.

Placing the elk softly on the ground, she checked the boy. He was breathing. Without wasting a moment, she hastened to check for a weapon on him.

If left on him, he wouldn't survive the night, she knew. Either she had to carry excess weight or leave behind the boy as an acquaintance. Thinking for a minute she made her mind and carrying both of them she walked once again and continued her journey.

Sometimes the destiny decides. And sometimes it is the smallest decisions that change your life. Completing the hike and carrying the boy to the chieftain, she left him with the oldest and tallest tree in the forest.

She placed him in the root feet of the chieftain and continued further carrying the elk to her kitchen.

XXVIII

Awareness came slowly as if the distant pinpoint of light he had been watching was trying to lure him up and away from the darkness.

He closed his eyes to make it all go away. But discovered his eyes wouldn't close, so he continued to watch the glowing pinpoint as it grew in size and intensity. He realised the glowing pinpoint of light was nothing more and nothing less than pure, undiluted pain.

"None can harm to whom the God shields," the words echoed in his tympanic membrane.

"Yes," Renil whispered, making the word audible, barely.

"Can you open your eyes?"

"No."

He might have said it, he really couldn't tell.

He felt the warmth of a person's breath against some part of his body, but nothing felt connected.

"Why not?"

"Hurts, leave me alone."

"What hurts?"

The boy tried to discern it all. It seemed like a voice, a woman's voice was responding to him, which meant he must make a sound.

The pinpoints of light in the shape of number eight were getting closer, fully taking the dimension and tone. Everything went brighter and the disc-like etching tool slashing eights made the intensity of light beyond the resistance.

"No!" he cried as loud as he could, trying to make himself heard, but the only sound that came out of his mouth was a raspy groan. The whirling disc lunged forward, unforgivingly, compelling his eyes to open in pain.

XXIX

The mid-morning sky was like a blue vault with frills of clouds and the sun pouring from the dome.

Darkness ebbed slowly, and his vision cleared. The branches were neither straight nor curved, rather more like arms waving at him, thin air tapping his cheeks gently and rowdy and firm support on his back, the trunk of the chieftain. He was sitting facing the ravishing stone house, a cottage maybe, he wasn't sure. It looked mysterious.

A small cottage perched on the plain within the woods, old and yet it seemed alive and welcoming, a warm ribbon of smoke rising from the old chimney. The walls are made of the same stones as the roof. The cottage was the only thing there. There were no other houses around it, and this one would have looked abandoned if not for the smoke.

In stupefaction, he rubbed his eyes and looked again. The pain got buried fleetingly as the view in front was mesmerizing. The arrangement was exceptional, made carefully combining the hues of the stones, the flowers, sods, saplings, bushes and shrubs producing an optical illusion. He. at last, realized it was a stone house, and the entire disposition was ingenious and natural.

Hunger got his thoughts back to his stomach. A shadow came from behind the tree as if reading his mind.

"Take this."

He looked up to the source of its casting. The face he saw was radiating sunlight like a mirror. She held galaxy in her hazel eyes, and the hair was red as maple. She wore a black robe covering her perfectly build figure and with her prepossessing hands she offered.

"Go on, have this, you'll feel better."

The soft brush of the hands in exchanging the saucer removed all his tribulations and without second thoughts he gulped from the cup offered to him.

By the time he finished, there went his saviour on her way to the stone house. Wiping his soup whiskers off from his sleeve, he placed the cup on his side and found a coyote fur jacket. He dismissed its relevance and thought about the woman he recently witnessed.

Her beauty was beyond words.

XXX

Joel was in the waiting chambers as he will help his friend no matter whether a formal investigation would be established about the homicide at the cabin in the farmland or not.

Sitting inside the clergy compartment, he checked his wrist for the arrangement of short and long hands. Quarter to ten. He had travelled far up north of the country in pursuit of the boy as his employer also his friend wanted him to find the culprit.

He had contacted the prayer's committee and fixed a small meet with the prayer mister at the headquarters involving no one from his office or police.

This was a personal mission for him.

There was no acquiescence in whether Joel could find the boy ever again, but his belief was strong. It was just a day past the Founder's Day, and he had time at hand.

He recalled being told invariably, no matter what the situation or the circumstances define, if and only if you have the conviction within, it shall fulfil your resolve. Don't let anyone or anything convince you why it won't work, you don't need that message to reach your subconscious, revoke it. The messages that should reach out to your inner self must contain all the reasons why it will benefit you and once mastered this practice, everything you believe, you can achieve any claim.

Coming back in the moment, he got up from his chair to receive the man in the white robe.

"Did you find what you were looking for at the ceremony?" he asked straightforwardly.

"Almost," the plainclothesman answered, taking back his seat.

"Tell me how I can offer help?"

The old man was the man of the cloth, and Joel was aware he had to be careful and concise. He moved in his chair lunging forward coming straight to the point. They have shared information about your journey back from the tower day before yesterday, the 10th of May.

And I would like to ask a few things.

"Go on. What about it?" the old man replied in a polite tone.

"I would appreciate it if you could please take me through it from the beginning till the very end in brevity, if possible," he appealed.

"I would love to but pardon me for my age if I miss out something," the reverend said with a hearty smile and his interviewer beamed.

He began, "I received your message to wait inside but it was of utmost importance for us to get going as they made a call from the headquarters ordering our earliest arrival. Something urgent had cropped up for yesterday morning with the minister of state. Leaving the tower from the back door, as usual, they cleared the lane for our speedy departure, and we made through the gates with no disorder."

"It was a comfortable ride," he mentioned making sure he recollected everything before he was to finish.

We halted thrice for food and fuel breaks on our way, and I believe we made it through the headquarters by the late evening.

'As brief as required,' he thought.

"And can I ask you one more thing with your permission?" he proposed.

"Sure, why not?" the man replied.

"Was there anything unusual during this journey?"

"Oh! At my age, nothing remains sensible," the old man laughed.

"As I said, it was smooth."

"Thank you."

He took the hands of the josser, smiled and thanked him for his time.

"May you find whatever you seek," the old man blessed him.

The doors to the chamber opened again. Deep down he was disappointed, thinking he wouldn't have to travel up north if the chip was receptive. But technology alone is not enough. The only guess he had made about the boy was that he must have had somehow sneaked in the sedan and escaped the tower, but there was not enough information to support what he guessed.

He walked outside the chamber.

The old man's voice interrupted his monologue.

The old man he was interviewing called him from behind.

"Oh, and son, when we left from the seventh road hilltop eatery, they call it 'The Terrace', our driver pulled over, almost as soon we started and closed the boot, so counting that we made four halts."

"Seventh road hilltop eatery," the Hawkshaw repeated.

"Yes, they prepare the best lasagne. They aren't famous yet but do try it if you go that way." the old man's voice faded.

'The Terrace,' he repeated to himself.

XXXI

The stone cottage covered with beautiful curtain creepers comforted him. The flowers were of every colour and glimmered from distance stressing the exterior of the living space that stood a front.

The cottage was a few yards from a hike in a combination of down and uphill. He understood it when he saw the human figure in cape cropping up in the line of his sight, moving towards the house. He recalled what encompassed him when he had entered the woodland and that differed completely from where he was currently resting.

The thickness of the mat of moss everywhere surrounding him typically grows in the dense green clumps of the forest. The taller and older redwood trees replaced the lean cedar trunks with healthier trunks. The open space between the greens, the canopy formed by a collection of individual plant crowns now included multiple horizontal layers of vegetation, representing a variety of tree species.

Even the size of woody debris varied, greatly.

His focus shifted back to the woman in the cape who had almost made her way to the stone house.

'Does she live all by herself?'

'A vigorous woman,' he thought.

The broth he had lately relieved his senses, and it made his eyes heavy and his headlight, settling on the mat of moss, he rested and dozed off.

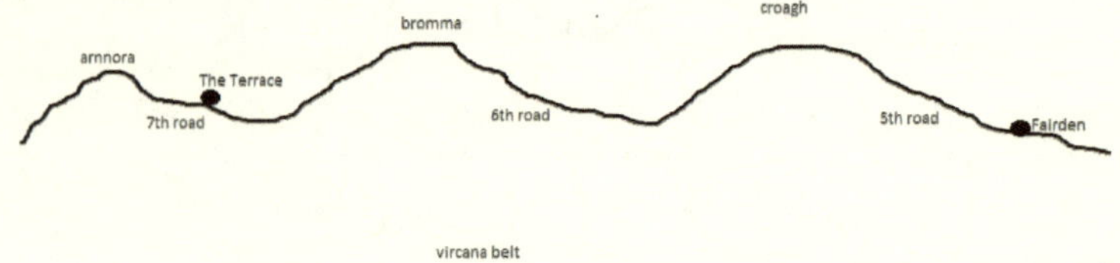

Map of the Vircana mountain range.

XXII

The rock arose from the ground as if it reached for the sky.

The peaks of the Vicrana belt sculpted by the raindrops of aeons, stretching for over four hundred vast miles, was the northern mountain range. They were green at their base, the forests namely Arnnora, Bromma and Croagh.

Wending this way and that, making tight turns that felt for the entire world as a fairground ride along the roads, were the important link to connect to cities and villages in that region of hills. As if gathered by nature's wand, the forests were at thirty to seventy miles or fewer from one another.

Three major roads made up of the mountain range, the fifth, sixth and the seventh road, all to climb up and down the mountain belt which was the north-eastern front and about 270 miles away from the city of Radena.

High up, every home was like an autumn leaf lying gently on the earth. Around them was the green of the trees and the road shining like silvery stems on a frosted late morning. The clouds moved in a breeze he couldn't feel if he was still wearing his suits, but he was no longer working officially and had taken a break from the formal wear.

The world below was so enchanting it was a privilege just to breathe the sweet air. It was long ago, he remembered, before he started working in the city, he had felt this kind of fresh air bustling through his lungs.

Sipping his coffee at the patio of the hilltop eatery of the seventh road, he felt a sort of homecoming.

Passing the square tables, glass tops, menus under glass tops, and the terracotta rustic tiled floor, he came back to his table which was next to the large window and called for the cheque.

Playing gently with the small vase of yellow carnation flowers on the table, he was listening to the classical music which was reverberating softly inside the eatery.

He looked outside the window towards the parking and saw a blue shabby hatchback. The man seated inside the car was eating his takeaway while staring at his table.

The server dressed smartly in his black and white gave the bill to Joel.

He checked the total and asked the server casually, "Is he regular?"

"Excuse me," the server replied.

"The man in the blue car," he whispered.

"Oh, forgive me, Sir."

He looked through the window.

"Yes, that's Mr. Jacobs, our regular customer. All his meals are with us. He loves to eat at The Terrace," the server continued.

He paid him and left the table.

Some folks have invisible addictions to tobacco, caffeine, or painkillers. But he was too obvious to miss. He wore it like a thick overcoat everywhere he went. Whenever a new server would serve him, he always complained, "The doorway to the eatery just not fit for people my size."

Joel waited for the man to finish his meal and then knocked on his window. The overweight man pulled down his screen only to half an inch and said in an annoying tone, "what do you want?"

He asked in a concerned tone "I am looking for my younger brother."

He was last seen around at this eatery, about a day or two days ago.

The man pulled down his windowpane as soon as he heard the word 'brother'.

I knew the boy was in trouble. His clothes were ragged, and he came out of the boot.

"Surely that's not a place to ride in," he continued.

I sensed him to be suspicious and followed him for a short while as he moved from the road into the forest.

Joel, supposedly the elder brother of his story, pleaded with the man to show him, if only the way, where his little one went.

He offered the sleuth a ride and the hatchback jerk started puffing some dust in the air before leaving for the road.

XXXIII

"Thank you, Mr. Jacobs."

He shook hands with the chubby man after a quick and short drive and left his shabby car. He gave a last wave to the settling particles off his face and pulled his water bottle from his bag, taking a sip from it.

He adjusted the torch in the upper pocket, the first zipper opened partially, and he took his rosewood handled camping knife from its deer-antler grip and pushed it inside his cargo pants waistband, for safety sakes.

He checked on his cell phone to confirm the time and adjusted his strap watch. The phone would not last long and so he switched off, sending a message to his employer:

"The reception of the device has failed, and I am not sure of the days it may take. My coordinates are 71°24'12.2"N 2°11'26.5" E."

He shared the long number displaying on his screen, tapped on the end option and switched off his phone. Placing it in his bag's inner pocket, he realized the phone was still active, and the notifications read similar coordinates, 71°24'12.2"N 2°13'26.5" E.

He glanced at the map and memorized all he could. The technology had finally worked. Swinging the sack on his shoulder he hurried to move away from the seventh road and into the Arnnora forest.

It was sunny, but he was entering an uninhabited land. The vast land stretched for miles with a few trees and patches of weed grown wildly. His hopes were soaring high despite being stranded because he knew this was his best chance for the findings.

In times of distress, think about the reason for induction, keep up with your resolve and ensure to fuel your subconscious with everything positive you can find – the words of wisdom from his master were his motivational travel companion.

What he was going through was not all that his job had made him, a few similar situations throughout his career made him the man of the calibre he was, with every addition to his inventory of investigations was an addition in his talent, but he always in his heart gave the credits of his merits to his wildling master.

He had never failed in delivering with his cases and that added to the reasons he was where he was.

The only person who can give you what you seek is your own self.

'What you have started, you must finish.'

Similar to the boy, Joel had a rough childhood and had learnt to sail through the privation of life the hard way, the difference however was he got abandoned by his parents.

He was just eight when his parents gave him to the orphanage with a promise to return in a few weeks, and that was the last he remembered seeing them. With the other orphans he spent the next nine years of his life and then one day, he just left.

Turning his back on the world, he left for the woods of Bromma with a resolve to never return. But what he did not expect was the turn his life would take, in a considerably brief period, in just a couple of years.

The walk he took back then was like the one he was taking now.

After all, the forest was of the same mountain belt. Pausing for a short while he scanned the surface coming back to the afternoon of the moorland and admiring the scattered flora, he observed the grassland and brushed the thoughts from the past.

He pulled out his phone for coordinates but in vain; the device gave a message, network lost. He would need his phone if not now, but later, and it was finally turned off.

XXXIV

The Fairden village was at the western tip, the end of Croagh forest, three miles off the highway road, the fifth road. It was the point where the fifth road meets its sister, the sixth road and territory markings of the forest region of Bromma begins.

He looked around and found himself alone in the mighty mountains. The curved road was snaking down, and the valley looked like an anthill from the top. He turned his gaze away from the thick cotton-like clouds onto the open road, which like a black ribbon over the highlands, disappeared into the horizon where earth meets the big sky.

The child stands so still, unsure if the road is friend or foe. Long hair blows about his face, obscuring the layer of grime that gets broken only by tear tracks. His clothes are of the wintertime that passed several weeks ago, and his cheekbones are more pronounced than they should ever be on one so young. At his age, he should be cherubic, but he looks poor and homeless.

The pain of being alone was too hard to endure, trying for nine years he finally chose the inner self, he always felt negative about where he lived as if there is something bigger destined for him something more than the small village of Fairden.

His parents had abandoned him for the reason he knew he would never know, and the orphanage never felt like home.

Young Joel gave his suffocated soul an escape.

But there he was walking on the highway road clueless, wondering what's next. Tears rolled down his cheeks once again. He picked a pebble and gave it a nugatory skip, throwing it far and beyond. The pebble bounced twice, and a thud sound shifted his attention.

The water softly running down through a large metamorphic rock lured him towards the inner curve of the isolated road into the woods. A strange pull got him going towards nature.

Bromma was one part of the mountains of Vircana, and the road cut through the mountain into the valley downhill in a connection for the national highway to meet the seventh road to the region of Arnnora.

Sliding through the crack of the enormous rock, young Joel slipped into the wild, unaware his life was about to turn upside down. Walking comfortably around the serene thicket of the woodland, he got adrift in nature and was already into the dense vegetation.

Despite being raised in the mountain regions of Croagh, the woodland mesmerized him. The hemlock, cedar and pines were exceptionally tall and the berries around the roots were differently coloured and tempting. He had his fill and stored as much as the little pockets of his pant allowed.

Walking a little more, he admired the beauty around him and then rested under a tree trunk, thinking about what he would do here.

He was thinking to walk back to the big rock and wait for transportation to pass through the sixth road or simply returning to the orphanage and making a solid plan before attempting an escape again.

What would be the repercussions of going back if returned? Did anyone even care that he had left?

He shrugged, ignoring the self-talk, and closed his eyes to rest. With a sudden sensation of spinning, he opened his eyes and felt alright. He closed his eyes, and the commotion returned. His head was stationery like a centre bore, and his body was spinning anti-clockwise like a wheel. The berries were wild. He felt nauseated they were inedible, he immediately realized.

Quickly trying to get up on his feet, he failed to hold himself and collapsed and everything around him revolved. Panic took over. He shook his head, jolting sideways and then quickly putting his fingers in his mouth. Trying to take out the consumed assortment, he coughed severely, but nothing came out through the food pipe. He tried again, pulling hard this time. More cough, but no results. He was choking and was getting short of breath.

It was a bad idea to escape. He cursed his instincts, and the dried tears started falling anew in helplessness. His body shivered and his pulse scooted. He saw his nearing death and all he could do was close his eyes. He was no more in control of his body.

Darkness...

The space he saw was a blank convex room, his body became light as a feather, the lungs contracted, cautioning him to breathe.

It was a tunnel, and he was passing through it like air, quiet, dark and so peaceful. His lungs were contacting steadily, reminding him to breathe. He ignored the alarm as he could see the light at the end of the tunnel now and he rushed towards the source of light, but his pace was pre-determined. Waiting for the journey to complete, he was admiring the source of light.

The lungs relaxed automatically, and a cool sensation felt through the body, finally numbing him, focusing back on the light he dragged to complete his journey but could not progress. The distance became stagnant. He tried again, but the tunnel collapsed from all the surrounding sides. He pulled but couldn't move any further. The tunnel was getting shorter with every passing moment, and soon he will get buried under the darkness.

The peaceful darkness was now claustrophobic, and the light was fading, fading to zero, to a dot a tiny speck. The struggle was fierce, and the darkness heavy, so heavy. His body shook, and the confusion bought him back to consciousness.

'Milk of poppy' were the words he heard coming back to life. A soothing sensation felt down the throat.

A compassionate voice whispered, requesting him to keep breathing. With partially opened eyes he saw an image, the pupil focusing slowly.

The cape was magnificent, brown coloured, long and plated, the face covered under a hood, and the snow-white beard outgrown from the hood. The figure in front of him felt like that of a sorcerer. He was his saviour, who would later become his wildling master.

The grassland in front was wild and wide. He woke up from the memory of the past. Rubbing his hands, he massaged the eyes before getting up and continuing his pursuit.

XXXV

A cup of shrubs soup was sumptuous to keep him asleep for the afternoon.

Bugs zipped in and out of his ears, humming and buzzing their little annoying songs. The forest hummed with life all around him. The air turning cold and the changing ambience around the chieftain woke him.

Renil looked towards the cottage with the hope to spend the night in a cosy place but wasn't sure of the direction. The woman, the habitant of the stone house, would she come back again to his aid?

He looked around himself to find anything that can keep him warm. Scarching within his proximity while sitting, he tried but couldn't find anything except dry leaves and tree barks. He had to get up and work, so he did. Near the chieftain and the area insight, he found some stones, stacking them along with the branches, wood pieces and the bark he made his way back to the tree trunk.

Looking again towards the stone cottage to imitate the design, he started with the preparation.

"A little dark to start," she smiled when she saw the boy through her window.

He was struggling with something. She observed him for a time and then dismissed her gaze and got back to placing the cape to the hook on the wall.

He kept scooping and scratching around the trunk, applying the combinations of the handful of articles he had got with him, and it assisted him to keep up with the temperature of the falling night. An hour had passed, and he got exhausted. Exhaustion was good, kept him busy and assured him he would sleep well.

"That's enough for a day," he exclaimed.

Not as comforting as he had thought, but it will keep him warm.

The fur jacket finally made sense to him and draping it around like a blanket he rested, feeling lost and confused. Pushing his hands inside the inner pocket, he found some dried meat inside the fur clothing. He was happy and certain. She will help him. He smiled, raising the snack in the air towards the cottage-like toasting the drink and then ate it.

He told goodnight to the chieftain and went to sleep.

XXXVI

He covered the cedar stretch in the afternoon after a quick nap and was almost at the brink of entering the dense part of it. Instinctively calculating the time, he guessed it would take about an hour and a few minutes to cover the moorland. Joel put his torch to work as it was dark and looked in his bag to grab onto the energy bar he was carrying.

Eating the assortment, he focused on his options.

He had been walking since early afternoon and after a very long and lone walk had settled in the treehouse where he was biting on his share of packed protein. He was on his own, but near to civilization as after walking for almost half a day he had found a few abandoned treehouses and the vast grassland which held the maple forest at its tip.

Frisking the boy before his way down the stairs in the tower, he had put the cashew sized, microphone like tracking chip on the inner collar of his shirt. He did not know the boy would escape, but diligence was his second nature. It was a secure way of tracking a suspect, a culprit. Felons are likely to flee in the first chance they get, and a tracking chip worked like their odour to sniff them out.

The boy could have been far away from the wild and had taken the highway road going back to city life, or else he was still wandering in the forest. Mr. Jacobs was not lying about the boy as the coordinates were from nearby, but the tracking system had glitches so he cannot completely rely on that technology.

Knowing that they would follow him, it would incline Renil towards the woodland than anyplace else, only if he was unaware of the tracker placed on him.

'What if he had identified the microchip?' he thought.

Then it was all beating around the bush, and a waste of life, but something inside of him told him the boy was struggling somewhere within the maples, the chip still tagged and coordinates he had seen were true.

He contemplated and gave himself a month to search for the boy in the woods, and if not able to find him, he would accept his fate and leave and tell his friend that he tried but couldn't help.

You have two lives, one when you realize that you only live once and the other starts after this realization.

The life you live should be a balance of compassionate and practical living.

Stepping out from the treehouse he started, he knew it was not late as it seemed, even though the shadows were drawn. It always gets darker near and around the forest, he remembered.

The moorland with the purplish sky up above held the heap of clouds and they ambled, making space to welcome the lunation. He understood it would not stay this beautiful.

Fireflies however were distorting his thoughts.

Happy to see some company after all the while and his hopes sparked bright but the fireflies cannot emit light at such wavelength.

XXXVII

The fire torches formed a straight line at the horizon and some human figures arrived. Despite being outnumbered, he was confident.

He laughed softly at the thought of fireflies.

With his even strides, hands oscillating around his waist and the palms outward-facing, he tried to send a message through the body language, an attempt to inform the intended sense of harmlessness from a distance. And within himself, he was preparing a strategy for his chance of survival. From the distance, it felt as he had disturbed some sort of celebration.

He looked for their leader while approaching the tribe. They raised fire torches higher and Joel was walking right into a disaster.

'Too late to be sorry,' he thought to himself.

With every approaching step the crowd cried louder than before, as a sign of warning to stop. He could gauge from the proximity. He was not only outnumbered but undersized to the average built of the forest people. They were strong and muscular. His chance of winning was rare but having experience in contact sport was worth the effort.

'Stay focused and concentrate,' he assured himself.

Clarity is the key remember, it gives you the purpose, and the purpose gives you the clarity, and this is where you find out who you are.

He continued with determination.

XXXVIII

The creature was huge and grotesque, with matted hair and huge twisting horns protruding upward into the dark sky. The contorted figure eclipsed the moon. He stood on its knotted haunches and howled as its wrinkled face stared at Joel. Far cries faded, and the passage made up of the crowd parted equally in two.

Giving off an aura of pure hate and evil expressed in its dull black eyes. It was an animal, a strong one, as huge as a bear, green eyes, devilish and blood-seeking. Its two horns were curled, the flesh was rotten to the bone, and the beast could take down anything that comes in his way.

Joel felt chills down his spine, and it almost made him abandon his mission.

'Never lose the initiative,' he reminded himself of his strategy. Keep moving and keep the enemy distracted.

He was at the front line, face to face with the beast, looking closely he tried to identify what creature was it. The light was falling directly on the giant and the thick facial hairs were visible. With heavy steps, it moved closer towards him. The vertical measurement of Joel was incomparable with the Horn Head, but his belief was larger than the leviathan. He was fearless, despite knowing his odds were bleak.

The two-legged beast was a human, and the horns were part of the masquerade. The appearance was the primitive tactic of supremacy for the people of the forest and that clarified to him, he was facing the leader of the wild horde.

He had to think of his feet of a strategy to save from doomsday.

A pre-eminent way to tackle any opponent is to make them winded, make them work and wait for an opportunity to strike and when you get one, strike hard – the words rewind in his head. He relived the lesson, recalling the day when he got briefed about the gigantic animals of the forest by his saviour. It was long before he started his city life before he became 'private eyes'. Standing his ground confidently, he faced the demon. Horn Head was within five yards proximity.

He realized the man was bigger than he had expected, and he could easily grapple him from this distance if he wished to.

Taking a subtle step back, he dropped his bag to the side, maintaining his distance.

The chief signalled the crowd, and the bodies moved a few steps backwards.

In a comfortable stance with a balanced core, he stretched his shoulder and neck and tightened his fists. He switched his footing forward and backwards and then became calm, taking in a deep breath, focusing on his energies and consciousness, prepping for his toughest physical test.

Controlling his breathing while looking over his surroundings and stepping back further, ensuring he was out of reach of the standing man-mountain.

He rolled down his sleeves and challenged the Horn Head to charge on and get him.

The madman lost it and came towards his prey, and it was this decisive moment when everything Joel had learnt, he must consider and use.

***

The Horn Head had grown older, but he was still a powerhouse.

He threw his body weight behind the fist that edged closer to his opponent's face. It hit the jaw with such force blood pooled into Joel's mouth. Pain erupted from the point of impact. The sleuth repaid this by punching the beast into the stomach with all his body weight. He dodged the tribal fist that followed and came up with his own; for a brief instant, the green eyes widened before the chief tilted his head back and slam it into his opponent.

He stumbled apart for a brief second to catch up before diving back.

"Is that all you got?" he crowed, smirking infuriatingly at the Horn Head.

The tribal blood hummed, and anger took over. With full swing he attacked, using both his hands to get to the little creature, but he was smarter than he seemed.

Joel observed the demon's strides through his line of sight. He dodged and rolled over to the right of the charging brute. The beast stumbled and crashed. It petrified the crowd as the Horn Head could not stand properly, but the challenger never touched him.

Everyone was astonished.

He was patient and in complete control of the action. The Horn Head was limping, the back of his left leg was bloody.

The little man smirked and tightened his knuckles. The leader was far from his people. Running towards the panting beast he made his next move, jumping on the heavy body Joel shifted his weight to the right and punctured the human neck with his fist. He annihilated the beast in a moment, and the horned mask fell to the ground.

The body of the beast dropped, dropping the jaws in disbelief of his people, and Joel stood up from his knees as the Horn Head slayer.

He turned and faced the crowd fiercely.

'But how on earth did he slew the Horn Head?' the crowd wondered.

He had planned a strategy before the duo began and executed it with exactness.

Rolling down his sleeves he had gripped his jack-knife from the waistband, then dodging the attack he put the weapon to use, a simple but significant trick of hand helped cut open the back of the knee of the ogre, decelerating and making him limp. Before he could improvise, Joel had planned his next move–puncturing the supple cervix. He used his camping knife not once but twice, and the gamble worked. He was cheating death after all, and everything is fair when it's about saving your life. Before the tribal would know, if they would about the weapon used in the duo, he would have been out of sight.

The people of the forest were wonderstruck by the spectacle, the Horn Head was history. They came running, concerned about their leader, and left the outsider alone.

He walked past them and continued to do so until he entered the forest, and the crowd became fireflies again.

He wondered walking in the middle of the night. Things which seem impossible are things which are just never tried and the simplest of resources can be of greater significance if used with applied knowledge.

The memory of prayer hall came before him, the oval face, brown eyes, hair falling on forehead, reflective shyness and innocence, the same face that had deceived him at the tower.

He cannot stay at one shelter as the uncivilized people of the forest were not trustworthy. They were barbarians, tribal, and they will hunt for him.

He had been standing at the deviation and instinctively chose the spoor to the redwood trees leading to the dense vegetation.

Pulling out the torch, he continued his walk into the darkness.

XXXIX

The morning colours of soothing lavender and brilliant amber merged into neon pink and peach sky, and the dew was his usual morning alarm from past few weeks. Stretching his stature, he sat upright. The efforts from last night kept his feet warm inside a small burrow and the fur jacket and the dried meat did the rest.

He looked at the cottage, and reverence replaced his hunger. The woman who had saved him, the beauty of the woods, was performing hand and leg movements with finesse as if walking in the air fighting an invisible opponent.

The sight was mesmerizing and intimidating at the same time.

He wondered if she was what she was because of the wild, or was this some sort of art she had gained over a period?

He wanted to be like her, self-reliant.

His feet moved towards the path downhill in admiration. The morning breeze was refreshing, the grass turned his feet cold, but his heart was still warm with the fire invoked from the sight of the lady in cape. Before he could realize it, he had made his way to stone steps leading to the downhill path to the cottage.

She looked at him from the distance and then got back to her routine.

The boy kept descending the root of mingled and moss-covered steps.

She observed the boy while practising her moves.

Nature has powers to heal the body, mind and soul and he realized the fact in that hour. He knew he would have to head back to the tree where he started from, but he had suddenly found a purpose of his life, to learn from nature, learn from the woman who had taken his heart.

There is a sense of kinship with the flora, of an ancient soul that stretches into everything that lives. He spent the rest of his day thinking about nature, breathing in every way it is possible to expand –his lungs, brain and soul.

XL

She checked on the boy from her window, but the chieftain was all by himself under the dark sky, dancing solo.

'Night saunter,' she gathered.

But he was right there next to the chieftain smiling in contentment on his hard work. Perseverance had been the key, and the oldest tree had helped him learn about this.

His self-made space and the final scribbling were worth the effort.

Bundles of branches were sacrificed for almost every day, and in a few days short of a month he had pierced the trunk, finally making his way inside the heart of the hoary tree of the forest. The carved flap was the curtain door to cover his burrow, the final finishing.

Building his abode was the most recent accolade of the past days. During his tenure, he learnt that breathing was the single most important aspect and controlled respiration was the essence of life energies.

The simple variation called the 'vase breathing' a touch of reverse breathing along with visualization was the technique that helped him to survive the wild winter nights. Just two or four rounds initially and then returning to the natural breathing cycle. It would not change the rectal temperature but will help you increase the temperature of your fingers and toes and you would survive for the night.

Apart from mastering breathing, he understood fighting skills, endurance, the activity of the woodland, navigation from celestial bodies, hunting small animals and survival instinct. He had learnt it all from his wildling friend. Long walks in the wood had helped him keep his athletic physique, and morning combat practice with wooden sticks made him reach his prime.

He had gained self-discipline it is the way to a high quality of life and a calm and composed living.

He was a street fighter, but what he learnt here in the woods was the fury of the wild. He picked up all this learning in about a lunation, around one month.

The butterfly counts not months but moments and had time enough.

It was true for him. Every day is learning in the wild. His brain volume had enlarged because exposure to natural surroundings and diet helped him to maintain focus, concentrate and amplify the psyche. He had started to look like a hunter.

Part Three

XLI

It was dark and difficult to scan, but not for her eyes. Feeling her dagger inside her cape, she continued skimming.

No movement, only the dry air touching her skin. She stood still, concealed behind a maple tree trunk a few yards away from the trail of shrubs. She heard the footsteps. Maintained and a slow walk of a seeker sniffing in search of its prey. The shadow of a man changed its path suddenly. He got spotted. She waited. The scent went fading in the direction opposite the cottage.

"No need to worry," Renil said.

He was standing right next to her, but she recalled telling him to stay inside. Not only did he ignore the warning but sneaked in without her catching a sense of it.

"The people of the forest," he continued walking back comfortably towards the chieftain.

Why she helped him when she first saw him was something only, she could tell. They knew one another just enough to smile at each other and wave. Then the lessons on hunting, cooking, and teachings about food gathering followed.

She had prepared and conditioned him to keep up with the harshness of nature. They spent time in the woods and slowly got to know each other, and by the time he had built his resting place inside chieftain they had become more than friends.

The thought held her in her spot.

She had slipped her heart into his pocket before she knew and there it will stay, safe and sound.

XLII

Joel looked for the North Star (the Polaris) and changed his path, following the moss around the trees climbing uphill and then formed a lean-to-shelter with help of the branches. The rabbit he had picked from the bushes on his way up would be sufficient nourishment to spend the night.

He had to wait for the night to settle and would start only by morning.

He familiarized himself with the wildwood and manipulated his markings to keep up his cover. Reminded of old times in his days when he had escaped the orphanage and ran to Bromma forest.

To ditch the recent raid, he went on the downhill path to the trail of shrubs, leaving behind marks on the tree trunks from his jack-knife. The people of the forest had fire torches and they would find the marking. But he was far from their reach as he had climbed from the alternate route uphill, assured they won't be able to find him, at least tonight.

He thought about the boy while lying down comfortably in his shelter. There was no legal investigation, yet he wanted to pursue him, to help his friend, for the sake of his friendship. Nor his esteem, neither his honour this was about bringing the convict to justice.

He kept fleeing within the forest all the while. It had been four weeks and three days since the tower incident. He gave only a month's time to himself, but there he was, still searching. The last he had checked on the tracking device was two days ago, and the tracking chip gave network issues but was still active.

He never came across the boy during his time in the forest, but something inside of him told him to continue finding within the maple wood.

Keeping up with life when it benefits you is easy, but the actual test is when you get going with life when it is not benefiting you anymore. It happens with the best of us always remember this and keep moving.

Shifting in his bed of paddy, the thoughts of his wildling friend who was also his teacher, and the memories comforted him to sleep.

XLIII

Away from the chieftain, Renil was walking north amidst the woods. The place had been his home for the past couple of weeks, but it felt this is where he belonged. He had learnt to keep off the wild animals and be part of nature.

The thoughts about his journey in the wild were playing in his head like a movie, his first steps in the moors, the joy of escaping the past, the liberation, the misery of getting lost, finding the woman in the cape, her beauty, her lessons, the learning and his destiny.

He succeeded in his endeavours of becoming self-reliant and had also evolved in personality. Life in the wild had supplanted his anxiety with calmness, his weak frame by his agile physique, his pessimist approach with optimist vision, and his self-doubt by confidence.

The only restoration he could never have been the love of his mother.

He learnt the art of living but there lies a lacuna deep inside his heart of emotions and the past.

When he thought about his mother, he looked skyward. She taught him that when someone dies, they become stars and from up above guide the way to their loved ones. Searching for her in the vault up above, he fancied the stars. He knew the laws of regeneration and degeneration of the human body and mind, and he was aware of the cycle of life and death, but some teachings are never contested, especially the ones given by our mothers. And he pretended as if her theories were true.

Hiking up, he again glanced skyward following the Orion and then settled at a large rock resting away from the thicket of trees in a full moon night.

Admiring the dark sky holding the sparkling spherical shapes he was with his mother in his memory lane.

He could see the belt of Orion all the three stars. His mother was up above looking at him, smiling back at him, being proud of him, she knew it was an accident, he never meant to hurt her, he had his belief which pushed him to do more and be more.

Like usual, today was no different and the hope that maybe one day he will get something more than the stars in the night sky got him going on his way back to his hideaway, to return another night.

Starting his walk westward, he had thought about his father. They never exchanged a word, nor have they had a relationship or an emotional bond, but the fact remained that he was his father. Only in his thoughts, they could be together, his parents and him, as a happy family.

Time flies over us, but it leaves its shadow behind. People always say life is too short for regrets, but it's too long. He wished he had a rewind button.

Picking up a few pebbles from the ground, he skipped them in the woods to brush off the thoughts of the past. One of it tossed and knocked at the lean-to shelter, suddenly waking up its occupant.

XLIV

All was dark and silent.

Joel put at his position, waited, and then looking upward ensured if it was from the tree.

'A wild animal maybe,' he thought to himself and allowed to let it pass. He only went for his torch as a defence tool. A beam directly hitting the eyes can instantly blind the best of nightly creatures, but he didn't put it to use as he knew he couldn't risk it, yet.

He waited quietly and patiently and focused where the canopy was thinnest, at the forest's edge in the clearing, and the stars and the bluish charcoal moonlight assisted his eyes to adjust. The woods were lovely, dark, especially at zero hours.

An owl was silently sweeping past and found its post on the perch of a redwood tree right above the lean-to shelter. The call of his song was like a four-note musical coming from above.

For all its serenity, there is always danger in the forest. Sitting upright, rotating his vision, he slowly navigated his sight eastward, then westward and surveyed his circumference.

Utter blackness of the night-time in the woods abated the black trunks, surroundings became apparent, the path was deepest brown, and moonlight was bleaching the stones within it. The silvery rays penetrated the dense canopy from above.

He continued the scan amidst small sounds of rustling bushes and the howl of the wind, which gently was breaking the silence of the after dark. He thought for a minute as if to risk on his hideout but waited before acting and patiently let the moment pass.

The silence returned shortly.

Pulling back in his paddy, he rested and continued to admire the mottled brown raptor with dark eyes and the yellow bill on its fluffy face.

Those eyes reminded him of the boy.

So close, yet too far.

XLV

Resting inside the treehouse built amongst the limbs of the chieftain, he was thinking about the city of Radena, the house he lived in, his classmate Cyrus, the explosion at the gas station, Parkview Street, the couple he killed, the prayer hall and finally the eyes, the ones which were of the deepest shade of richest earth, got drilled into him before he ran from the prayer hall, he'd never seen such dark eyes with so much light in them. He knew the man was a hunter and he could have sniffed him out from the bottom of the earth if he had not fled in time.

His life girdled by nature now, he was thankful as he was in a completely changed and untraceable environment.

A soft voice echoed in the wooden space breaking his chain of thoughts and lifting his head he acknowledged the source. Stepping inside the holt, she ducked at the entrance and covering the ground slowly and cautiously she came next to his lair. He tapped the floor with his hands and shifted in his paddy, making space for her to sit.

She lifted the cape to nestle on the ground exposing a part of her radiant skin and his heart skipped a beat looking at her beautiful blooming feet, trying his best to ignore it, he looked skywards but his eyes kept ditching his mind.

It is a beautiful abode-she admired looking around the cosy and compact space. The walls being the inner side of the tree were the perfect canvas to exhibit his artwork and sketching skills.

Touching the wall, she felt the wings of the simple and winsome cedar waxwing drawn, the fawn colour of the inner side of the tree imitated the original field marks of the upper part and crest of the passerine and the bird mask scrapped black by the artist who was lying next to her. Next to the bird was a greyish brown mule deer buck with branched horn sniffing oestrus doe.

"The rut season," she asked, looking at him. He nodded in agreement to the hazel eyes that looked at him in the same admiration as his art.

Letting down his defensive instinct, he could feel the vulnerability like the buck drawn on the wall, his thoughts running wild on the beauty of her perfect body and her sharp facial features. She could feel his vibes and reciprocate within the blinking of her eyes like an approving doe. The exchange continued for a moment, and everything went still.

Renil could feel a strange yet strong pull from the girl sitting next to him and the way she touched her maple red hair made him shift his weight to sit upright but before he could apply any force to change his position, she put her hands on his chest comforting him back to his lying position and kissed his mouth softly, leaning on him. He felt her round hips with his hands and gently squeezed on the butt cheek and kissed her.

The most beautiful creatures he had seen and observed were nowhere close to her charm, the fullness of her breast pressed against his upper body eased his mood and filled him with a sensation of the missing love.

XLVI

Signalling to his fellow-clansman, he directed him to cover the chalet from the opposite side. Nakoda, the rope keeper followed the instructions and moved away, leaving the manhunt party reduced to two and taking with him the glutinous threads he was holding.

Hiute – the bowman and Peoria, the weapon keeper, waited for Nakoda to take his position.

Putting pressure on the upper part of the mouth making a clicking sound, he affirmed his position was on point. Promptly behaving to the sound, the bowman looked at his partner and showed him with a hand sign to move forward.

Rushing towards the carved entrance, Peoria opened the creeper curtain with the pointed tip of his wooden shaft weapon while Hiute surveyed the exposed inside of the scullery from the archer's angle, looking through the small ledge on which his arrow rested, while aimed.

The chalet was empty.

They could see the fireplace along with the unfired earthenware stacked around an oval tub on the floor, alongside was the tan skin of a small mammal, the dried meat stored on a drying rack.

"Rabbit meat," Nakoda drooled.

The markings on the hemlock around the trail of shrubs aided Joel to ditch the raiding tribal party searching him, but eventually lead the hunting party to the empty stone cottage in which the three men were presently fighting over the belongings of the house.

The two men were tugging over the neck rest, the wooden curved tray fixed on a vertical and rectangular support base, ending with a hemispheric hollowed out base with symmetrical lines as it was a three-in-one tool – a stool – and it also could sharpen the knife.

Wrecking the inside of the food area followed by the living space, the party scattered in search of things they could loot. Reaching the room with the window, a cape caught Hiute's attention. Picking up the black piece of cloth, he smelled it through his pierced nose and calculated on the essence.

Turning around towards the aperture on the wall, he saw a broad tree, the broadest in the region. Leaving the cloak as is, he went to the kitchenette again and ordered his fellowmen for an immediate hike to the chieftain.

Before putting the fire torch to work, the looting party gathered the meat, the furs, and some stoneware and wrapped it through in the viscous braiding, leaving the cottage to burn through the wintery night.

Hiute walked towards the tree in agony, and the two men followed.

XLVII

Holding from the beautiful long fingers, he moved the hand resting on his sternum, softly placing it on the toned thigh partially covered with the black robe. She moved a little and settled in her position without opening her eyes.

Using one of his hands as a pillow and putting his head on it, he thought about the moments he recently spent with the gorgeous woman lying next to him. Her full lips were touching him a few moments ago while her scarlet hairs were falling on his face and the fragrance from it adding to the desire of wanting her.

His saviour was his lover now, exactly what he always secretly wanted, but he never thought would come true. She was beautiful beyond words and there was so much more to her than her skin-deep appeal that had captivated his heart.

Her words: 'Nothing can dim the light that shines from within.'

The first time she helped him get up from the ground when she had body-slammed him, teaching the knowledge how to disarm an opponent, he recalled.

She worked on him all these weeks, simply succouring and culturing him for the woods.

The love lesson he prayed she would give him each time he looked into her chromatic eyes finally offered to him this night.

A smile separated his lips apart, and he looked at her with contentment. She had given him protection, knowledge, subsistence, support, courage, self-confidence, strength but her name is the only aspect left, he reckoned.

He shifted in the grass paddy lying on his right flank, his head relying on his right elbow, supporting his head with his hand to have a fuller view of the pearl face of a nameless goddess, his first love.

Her neckline chiselled, and the pendant was falling to the side. He held it in his palm an azure blue semi-precious gemstone. Admiring it for a while, he focused back on her lovely face. Using his first finger and thumb, he picked the maple red strand of hair falling from her cheekbone and pushed it back behind her ear. She shrugged in happiness, half asleep.

As strange as it may seem, he had never asked her name, so she had never told.

"I'll be back," he whispered and left, picking up his coyote fur jacket, dressed, and moved outside.

***

With the bodily fluid watering the plants and the moss in the backyard around the chieftain, he felt the chilly winds with a tinge of warmth which was atypical in the middle of the night. Reasoning to it, he examined the night sky to comprehend the natural rhythm of darkness and light from the moon, but it balanced the natural cycle.

The meandering air currents in the atmosphere, the jet streams also impact the fluctuations in air pressure. Westerly winds and their pattern aid in weather forecasting in the north. The wildling sleeping inside the treehouse had told him.

Finishing, he gave a last gaze to the starry midnight blue sky in the black conical patterned canopy formed by the surrounding trees. He was returning to his lair to continue lovemaking but before it, he would pursue her name.

A sting felt on the side of his neck beneath the ear. Ants and mosquito are common in the woods and tried plucking out the carpenter ant of the maple. Brushing his neck with the back of his hand when he realized it was a petite lean arrow shot at him, a sensation of numbness spread to his limbs before he could complete the extraction.

A wooden projectile, a dart, he confirmed and the tip of it was slimy and coloured differently than the barrel and the shaft, before he could look for detailing his vision blurred, keeping his respiration controlled he tried to push forward in his natural way of the walk and turned and headed to the chieftain, creating a false sense of target miss for the unknown shooter.

The hunting party of three waited behind the cover of conical pines, watching the coyote furred deal with the blue rocket (aconitum). Peoria hanging the flute-like weapon back from its boar skinned strap beamed in pride, looking at his struggling prey while Nakoda patted him with his gigantic hands.

They derive the blue rocket commonly known as the queen of poisons from the perennial plants locally known as the wolf's bane.

His knees were getting weak with each step and he tried to keep his focus, but the sting was poisonous, making it difficult for him to concentrate. The fatal aconite can kill instantaneously, but Hiute ensured that the bow gun shooter keeps the dosage mild, advising him to apply more of tree gum and spit than the juice of wolf's bane.

The paralyzing effect of the semi-saturated blue, purple flower's juice had reached the cardiovascular feature of his body. He only wished if he had asked the name of his saviour before he left and could have called for help just for one last time, but it was too late already. His abdomen burnt and breathing became taxing. He got rid of his coyote jacket and rubbed his hands for better stimulation of blood in the body. Sitting down on the cold grass, he focused, but confusion had taken over with passing minutes. He could see the thick smoky clouds of grey colour emerging from the stone cottage in the far front mingling with the stars, and the abode of his lover was in flames.

Three human figures appeared from the burning background, validating the unusual warmth and the next moment he felt weightless and passed out.

XLVIII

The stones clonking alarmed him and he quickly took his cover behind the tree, keeping his palm gripped around the deer-antler weapon on his waistband. Joel waited in apprehension, holding his lean-to-shelter.

He got convinced the people of the forest might have spotted him and the disturbance earlier that night was not from an animal.

Another heavy sound of impact followed a monstrous one, from a fair distance considering by the echo of it. He knew he was safe by at least fifty feet as the minimum distance to hear an echo was to such approximation, but in the north, due to winter weather, the distance could be more than what he thought.

Relaxing his grasp to the reason, he immersed in the pine's canopy, hemlock and maple and concentrated. The sky behind the trees was smoky and grey, and the sight of the glow of fire came from the west.

The forest didn't have such fires. He was sure and even if accidentally there was one, it would not be at this hour, chilly winds eliminated wildfire. The only way to determine the reason behind the induced open fire was to follow the smoke, picking up the bag he ditched the shelter after dismantling the ridge pole and spars, abolishing its presence and moved downhill quickly towards the trail of shrubs, cautiously, leaving behind no imprints to pursue.

Darkness cloaked him, he continued striding parallel to the visible emission, allowing his existence only known by a flash of light from his pocket-sized handheld torch. Soon the torch became worthless because of the scintillating fire, and he took his jack-knife out from his pocket and back in his hand. He observed the heat, and the suspended sparks in the air and advanced towards the smoke.

The heat waves mixed brilliantly with the cold of the night as if an enormous bonfire and he looked comfortably through the shrubbery of the stone house draped in fire, slowly turning red hot and melting down in the gelid hours of darkness.

He could see an enormous tree standing tall, enjoying the warmth from the searing cottage on the far end.

He moved towards the tree and the fire in anticipation.

XLIX

The fire and warmness were weakening, and the ground beneath was drifting away from him. Chorus of delirium went on staggering and flushing him out of his wits, but a sensation on his tongue, an elixir, kept him safe from convulsions and the darkness. The taste of it compelled him to keep his mouth working and the round substance which felt like a berry kept his heart beating steady and controlled the sweating.

His eyes opened to a strain on his belly, but the jerk made him comfortable again. Hands hanging in front life-less and big leg muscles alternatively oscillating was all he gathered, he was surely being transported.

A heavy male voice whispered the letter K and number 27 and before he realized he was lying on a cold stone, a rock maybe. A firm pressure felt under the collarbone, in the hollow at the side of the breastbone. The point technically is a potent pressure point for addressing cardiac issues.

It was a pressure point of the body that maintains a fluid balance in the body, opens the chest, and relieves chest pain, chest tightness, palpitations and anxiety. It helps to promote the immune system functions and enhances natural energies in the body, improves overall health and reduces general weakness. He had read about it, or maybe he was told, he couldn't recollect. His saviour, the lady in her cape, had come to his rescue yet again.

'But why did her voice abruptly change to become manly?'

He tried to pay attention, opening his eyes, but before he could fully open them, he felt weightless. The ground beneath drifted again.

Renil could pick up three distinct male voices.

The sound of the cape lady was unique and recognizable.

'Was she silently following him or leading the male voices?' He tried to notice.

The oscillation made his head heavy, and he did not worry about his surroundings.

"He could run away all this while, but no one can get away from us." the voice boasted.

"I would smash his head at the same place where he killed our father and relish his blood in the drinking horn," the heavy voice continued with a smirk.

'Not a rescue for sure, a manslaughter, maybe,' Renil reasoned to himself, slipping back into darkness.

L

Chieftain got warmer despite the wood bark curtain being partially drawn. The paddy was the source of insulation inside the treehouse however it could not regulate the warmth to the extent she experienced. Something felt wrong.

She checked to affirm if she was all alone in the tree chamber, tapping softy around the paddy looking for her partner, but young Renil had left a long time back.

Pulling on her robe, she dressed quickly and tied her hair in a bun and left. She took her poniard out of its scabbard, ducking her way outside the carved wooden opening and stepped in the wintry eve.

The symmetry was brilliant, and the perfectly curved trail was glowing. The view became comprehensive in the far sight where the cottage was blazing to ashes. Her abode was aflame, the chalet was falling to the ground under the starry night.

She spent eight lunations and countless nights considering arrangements for ventilation, drainage, kitchenette and water reservation. Every stone, sap, tree, plant and flower were handpicked and nurtured. The window, the wooden door entrance, the inner walls, the tree-house chamber, the bed of paddy and the wooden furniture was self-carved and built. All of it was adding fuel to the fire, in her moment of reminiscence.

A tear rolled down her cheek she controlled her emotions and screened the surroundings moving her attention away from the sight of destruction.

The air abruptly exiled her lungs, and she felt winded, like a blow to the stomach.

She put her weapon to use just in time, moving the sharp tip of it behind her back, pointing it at the pelvic of her attacker. Gripped around the neck, she felt muscular forearms, muscles getting tightened. She got groped from behind. The weapon pushed deep. She pierced it through the skin and continued to push it further, but the grip didn't change.

Forest people were tough, but not beyond anatomy. She battled the thought and restored to push the dagger deeper into the skin. The attacker didn't respond well to the blade. She was penetrating the clothing, the animal skin worn by her assailant. The weapon was pointless.

Breathless, but the grip remained tight. The weapon was slipping off her hand slowly because of the pressure on her windpipe, trying to jerk her body fitfully for the last time, but it was physically too strong to outmanoeuvre. She thought about the boy. She wished if he was there; he had grown stronger, and he might have saved her.

Those brown eyes of his, black hair was falling on forehead, when he had met her the first time, from teaching him about everything he desired to survive the forest to the warm fur jacket, her first gift to him, it all flashed before her eyes. She could smell it profoundly as if he was next to her looking at her last moments.

Her last word was loud and clear, and it was the name, name of her lover:

"Renil."

The name had a magical effect. She felt eased to nearing death, could breathe ordinarily, the grip loosened on her. The numbness diminished as the diaphragm was stretching down to help pump air back into the lungs.

The most powerful antidote to death is love. Wintery wind blended with the warmth of the weeping cottage and her body was weightless, floating. Everything became calm.

Bliss in form of darkness, death was a sweet pleasure. She felt the relaxation, saw herself standing outside her cottage smiling and waving at the chieftain, and the black curtain was smoothly falling from up above. The fallen curtain bought with it an absence of colour, the unknown, she was waiting patiently for death to embrace her fully, the pitch-black space was expanding and it hauled her into the spiral, the closing scene of her life.

He blessed her before the last knot made on the neck chain, she remembered, leaving the little stone to rest on her chest and then kissed her on her forehead. It was one of the most sought-after stones, deep, celestial blue called lapis. This is the symbol of royalty and honour, God's power and of his vision, she was told by her father – she was back in her childhood memory.

She gave her neck pearl the last touch before her last breath.

LI

Many people lost their lives as they were reluctant and naïve because they did not leave the forest of Bromma despite the water level rising and paid the price. Arnnora forest was not the original habitat of the tribe, only a few who had survived the great flood knew. The people who outlived the flood buried the story so the people can stay united in peace and harmony for the years to come and do not seek ways to get back to Bromma.

The calm approach and the strategy to evacuate was what had won the heart of the men and women of the jungle who survived, and in return for their lives being saved, they offered him their loyalty and named him the chief. He helped the clan and guided them along the way to a new habitat, the Arnnora forest on the other side of the Viracana belt.

Zephyr was the name given to him by the people of the forest.

His face, long and heavy, and a snow-white beard, covered in hood reflected life experience and wisdom. The eyes were cerulean, and the face was wrinkle-free. The essence of longevity was intact as if he knew how one could pause the ageing. Strongly built and as tall as the people of the forest, his mere presence resonated bravery and confidence, the face was vibrant, as calm as a lotus resting in the water garden.

He was their chosen leader. The tribe unanimously gave him the title, except for the one named Maska, named after his heavy voice. He was the strongest of them all and thought he was the rightful chief of the tribe.

Maska envied his tribe commander, for he could never be as brilliant as the latter, but he wanted the status of the chief by any means.

Zephyr spent most of his time practising silence and appreciating the people and activities of the tribe.

He was a true master, self-reliance and self-satisfaction oozed out of him and attracted everyone he used to meet and teach.

People had a belief he was someone special who possesses supernatural power, a man ahead of his time.

The focus areas of his lesson were breath awareness, mindfulness and awareness about one's existing surroundings. He also conveyed about transcendental meditation, focusing on repeated words and series of words, observation of celestial bodies, the study of stones and gemstones, reading animal behaviour, nutrition and balance between hard work and sleep.

His vision was to create a society that helped one another to remain in peace and harmony and constantly challenge each other to attain a higher level of consciousness and well-being. The tribe revolutionised not because of their genes or evolution, but because of the practices they followed and the lifestyle they chose with their leader.

The flora and fauna were better than their prior abode, and the surrounding also contributed to the growth of their physical and mental stature. But the progression didn't last for longer than two decades.

Maska throughout his tenure kept patience and secretly plotted with his sons against the one he hated.

The chief was simultaneously working on rebuilding the land once home to people in Bromma forest. With the sprouting population, he knew they expected more space to sustain and flourish. He told his people he was working on a personal project and to gain spiritual growth he had to seclude himself from his responsibilities and duties for three lunar cycles every year and would return on the fourth full moon each winter.

"The body is a magnificent gift given to humankind, and the brain is the most sophisticated tool to guide it. One can only employ it superlatively when withdrawn," he told his people.

He identified Maska and his jealousy, and to put it to better use, he nominated him as the chief in the duration of his absence.

Accepting what they offered to him as a delegation, he never let his emotions take charge of his actions and he heartily conducted his duties towards his people as their delegate. The tribal deputation continued over seven years and on the fourth full moon, that year news came about the death of their leader.

The message about their leader's demise brought deep sorrow in the people of the forest and this was precisely the moment Maska had been waiting for. He assured the people that he would avenge the death of their beloved, late chief.

The deceased had named Maska the leader in his absence and the respect they had for the bearded chief led to the submission of their reasoning and will against the then strongest man of the forest. Nobody knew how their leader died, but Maska claimed it was the herd of oxen that killed him.

To prove his valour, he killed an entire herd of oxen from the moorland and made a crown out of their horns and proclaimed himself as the Horn Head.

LII

A crisp and clear voice softly echoed, "Wake up."

A commotion across her facial muscles confused her. It continued, followed by the voice repeating, "You are fine."

"Wake up."

Subtle push she felt on her breasts with the warmth of air pumped into her lungs. The process repeated in quick successions and with a flood of pins and needles sensation, the tips of her arms and legs which were limp came back to life.

The reddish-brown colour surfaced when her vision settled. A robe with its inside covered in a whitish colour of fur, she gazed with her half-opened eyes. It was the coyote's fur jacket. She thanked the Gods she wasn't a hostage and continued to browse upwards. Her eyes closed from exhaustion. The respiratory system was picking up, she could feel and remain in her position.

After a pause she opened them again and found the coyote fur with his back turned on her, setting up a small bonfire.

"Renil," she whispered.

She cleared her throat to call him again. Sitting on her hamstrings, she looked at him.

"Renil," she tried harder.

"I am sorry," she heard the reply.

He had found the fur jacket on his way to the chieftain and had kept it.

The man sitting in front of her was not who she thought him to be. In a moment's blink, she realized, and before she could check for her poniard, the voice proactively replied.

"You'll need some rest, don't be harsh on yourself."

"We will pursue him first thing tomorrow morning and I know where he might be."

She knew he was not one someone from the forest but then who was he?

And why he spared her life.

He looked like a hound, but a calm one. She might have seen him before, maybe in the dark, but she was not completely sure.

LIII

They walked downhill and away from the trail of shrubs towards the dense part of the wildwood to reach for the tribal territory.

"It won't take long from here," Joel said, breaking the silence.

"You are right," she added softly, speaking for the first time to the man who tried to choke her to death last night.

"I know this route well."

"I hiked this path three and half weeks ago," he continued.

His jawline squared, clean face and the eyes dark as a hound but from the body language he seemed harmless and unusually calm, he carried himself with defined authority and prudence, and his physical stature, athletic, shoulders were broad and robust. He looked like a hunter.

"I am Joel," he introduced himself, breaking her chain of thoughts and the awkward silence.

"I am Uliana," she replied.

He looked at her and smiled.

The beautiful woman walking by his side seemed like a familiar face. If not for her slim, small nose and arched eyebrows, her face would not be feminine, nothing overly fine or eleven. Her features were pronounced with more of fatherly inheritance, yet she was simply beautiful.

"At the tip of the forest, the vast land is the tribal camp," she changed the subject of conversation.

"What is it you want from the boy?" she assertively asked.

He killed three innocent people and ran away.

"And you are the authority that punishes such doings?"

"You can say so."

She had guessed at the first sight looking at the boy he was running from something, but she had never asked him about it.

"How are you so sure if it is him behind such an undertaking?"

"Basis some evidence," he replied confidently.

"I am not sure how long you have known him, but he is a convict," he added.

"So, it's between you and him, the seeker and the hider," Uliana responded.

"I respect whatever it is you share with Renil, but I want to make it clear I will take him back."

"It is not him I made this far. I am here because they burnt my house and looted my belongings while I was away."

Feelings are like temperatures. Attraction is warm, curiosity is warmer, anger is boiling, hate can torch, but it can also freeze. Love, well, that's a temperature best left under neutral.

They both continued talking about the boy, about what had happened in their respective encounters with him.

Through the dense part of the forest reaching for the quick hike uphill, the two halted to find the human figures on the horizon celebrating their fiesta.

LIV

The fire was burning sweetly and softly, cooking the meaty elks from beneath – the preparation for the jamboree. The songs were being hummed after intervals.

The evening was approaching, and the sun was setting down on the moorland.

The prisoner tried to fiddle with the cuff braid of ropes but didn't pursue it for long. He knew the man, who had splashed ice cold water on him, he was the guard who was keeping a watch on him.

A little girl came running towards this man followed by a few more children who then collectively requested the guard to bend down as they wanted to tell something important. The prisoner tried to give an ear too.

"They are on their way," the children whispered.

The man replied with a nod and smiled. He ruffled the hair of the little informer who broke the news and hushed the kids. The bunch ran away playfully into the crowd and shortly after, he could hear the neighing of horses. The man seeing the horses lifted Renil back on his feet and cut loose the ropes that had been troubling him all afternoon.

Jerking his arms as they finally pulled apart. He opened and closed his fists to circle the blood back into his fingers and palm, then rotated his neck slowly and then stretched and comforted his shoulder and back muscles. He finished his quick stretch and noticed the crowd was gathering and the mass of people had encircled him.

The man who had cut him loose was drawing lines on the ground, which appears like two square boxes. He could feel an outline was being drawn to identify where he was standing. The guard had moved towards the elevated frame and was completing the square outline around it. He stands no chance against the tribal, the people of the forest and their ways of handling outsiders.

Everyone fell silent as soon as the man sketching the lines finished. Then he moved towards the cooking fire and lit up the fire torch. The simple sound of horse's steps followed, a party of three men came running towards the crowd on their horsebacks. The tribe far cried, and the fire torches moved from hand to hand, lighting up the entire vast land in the circular formation.

Renil knew he would not see another day.

LV

"Are you ready?"

"Yes, I am," she said fiercely.

"You would need it," he flipped the scabbard out from his shoulder bag and threw it towards her.

Catching her poniard mid-air, she swiftly placed it on her waistband where it belonged, and she smirked.

Pulling up her cape hood, she moved away from Joel and carefully camouflaged into the expanse. The sleuth marched straight towards the circle of fire. He had been through this before, a déjà vu, but he was lucky the first time.

If her assumptions were true, this plan could be their only chance at saving the boy.

But it involved a bigger risk in following what was told to him from the cape lady who sheltered the boy.

He walked linearly into the territory of the people of the forest.

The crowd was busy with the actual spectacle for the evening, they shall serve the boy as a side dish at the supper with the charcoal smoked elks.

Unswerving circle of fire was a thicket of human bodies, on one side were the cooking fire pots and the slow-burning elks, on the other side, an arrangement in a straight line had the fire torches lit over a vacant space with a man, the keeper of three Hamdani horses.

Joel was walking towards the ring, briskly when the tribal shouted out loud raising the torches, showing the duel had begun. His walk changed to a jog and soon he was running towards the riot.

LVI

The woodcut chair on the elevated platform finally got taken. They lit up the quadrangle as it charged the clan with enthusiasm.

"It was time to serve the retributive justice to the people of forest."

A stout middle-aged man got seated on the chair and to his side were two men who appeared to be his brothers. One was clean-limbed and gracefully thin; he held an extremely slim but strong flute-like weapon on his shoulder. The other one was muscular, broad-shouldered and sturdy he was a mad dog waiting for orders from the chief to rip apart his prey.

Sipping from his horn-shaped flagon he demanded, "Tell my people who are you."

The crowd roared and raised their torches and repeated, "Tell him."

The boy was speechless. He tried to gather his wisdom as his silence could prove to be his nemesis.

"I am Renil," he replied with conviction.

The recently appointed chief, spitting his drink halfway down his throat replied, "Filthy little bug. How dare you to come to our land?"

"You murdered my father and disappeared in the darkness of the forest thinking of us as fools. Now you see what it got you into, you twat."

Short of words, Renil could not assimilate what on earth was going on.

"And let me tell everyone about your little trick – using your weapon in the duel, you bastard."

With a slight of hands, he used the knife, used with precision in the heat of the moment. The weapon was sharp enough to slash the tendon at the back of the knee.

"What was it, a blade?"

"You put a blade, a dagger in my father," he stood up from his place in rage with his face blood red, the big pierced nostrils expanding and contacting and his body quivering in pique.

He threw his flagon in disgust and rose his finger towards the boy saying, "You're dead."

"Payback time," he signalled his brother standing on his side to attack.

He knew the man-mountain Nakoda was more like a cat than a snake, and instead of killing fast, he would toy with his food.

"Kill the boy," the words his brawny brother and the crowd had been waiting for.

All roared unanimously, "Get him, get him."

LVII

The disc-shaped arena was nearby. She quickly crossed the cooking section and moved from behind the elevated platform towards the other side of the crowd where the horses got secured.

The keeper was more interested in the duel as the crowd was roaring in excitement and frenzy. He could not see the contact sport from the distance and curiosity was taking better of him. He scanned his radius and moved away from the fodder eating odd-toed ungulate mammal moving closer to the real extravaganza.

The bull amongst men Nakoda was trying to corner the little piece of meat, his hands were open and circled his broad chest, the horse keeper punched his knuckles in his palm cheering, "Get him!"

The mad dog leapt onward as if he could hear him. He jumped to get the hare, but the timely somersault dodged the beast.

"Ho!"

The tribe booed in unison.

Renil was eluding King Kong, staying away from the lunatic. His best chance at survival, but to tire his opponent would not be easy. They forced a wooden stick into the ring to make the spectacle more exciting. The giant banged his chest and howled, turning around he charged towards the boy.

The attacker tried again, this time leaning his back to reduce the margin of space for the somersault.

Renil dived between the legs of Nakoda and avoided merely by an inch.

"Oh!"

The tribe booed again in unison.

He was aiming for the wooden stick to improve his chances to fight for longer and gain some edge.

The keeper of the horses had covered some ground in animation and eagerness and was sauntering towards the circle of fire. A stone stumbled his feet, and it reminded him of the horses. He turned around for a nippy look at the animal and his eyes met a pair of killer hazel eyes. He felt something in his gut. The tip of her steel pressed against his navel, it passed through his intestines and made its way through the back muscles puncturing everything that came in contact. And it came back with the same precision making him fall, instantaneously.

She caught him before he could complete the fall and dragged him to the bushes next to the horses. Then mounting the mighty black horse, she manoeuvred the bridle and reins, making the horse canter towards the luminous ring.

LVIII

Reaching the brim of the sphere, Joel threw his bag and rushed. He was snaking his way through the crowd of tribal, constantly pushing to make space and penetrate the big-boned humans around him while they were busy with the dog and the bone game.

He paced, gripping everything that he could hold to advance and reach the tip of the circle. The fire was intense and the harsh heat waves were experienced from a distance. A huge monstrous figure was running feverishly, trying to catch onto its prey.

The body dodging the demon was athletic as a teenager, same steady but slightly ironic gaze, his brown eyes were searching for a cover from the beast, his sweaty black hair jumped in the humid air. The boy had not grown drastically, but he looked a little different from last time.

The tracker had produced a true reading.

Flames of fire and a beguiled past separated them.

Joel was just a few yards away from Renil.

Patience always pays off.

The flames changed their course, throwing all in despair. A sudden dust storm spread across the moorland rapidly. Everyone had to turn their back on the sport because the fatal flames and dust mixed with it moved in all directions. The dark figures were moving inside the ring, their forms visible but not their actions.

Filling his hands full of the ground dust he threw it straight into the eyes of Nakoda, blinding the beast momentarily and then hastily searched for the shaft that got aimed at him from the Sachem's spot.

Hiute had told his brother Peoria to use his flute-like weapon and shoot the boy as he was getting frustrated with the chase game. But Renil somehow steered clear of the blowgun dart because of the gust in the wind.

He rolled to his side where the shaft lay with its tip gooey and purple. The giant battling for his vision got stabbed by the blowgun dart, missing his neck, but the beast was quick to respond. He swung his enormous arms in the air frantically and the boy missed his target.

He got punched in the face and went flying to the ground.

Dark clouds were spinning slowly around him, and silence followed.

The lethal weapon was already in the hands of his attacker, he had missed the neck but had pinned the shaft in the beast's shoulder. Nakoda was rubbing his shoulder blade when their eyes met. He trashed the shaft and laughed at the little boy.

The monster was walking afresh towards him.

He was sure that they poisoned it, but the muscular man was immune.

Nakoda was now in proximity to the boy, and he raised his arms to reach out to kill his prey and gripped him from his throat. Lifting the boy in the air, he laughed at the helplessness of his prey.

"You're done."

***

Squall lasted only for a few minutes and the figures came back in sight, followed by their actions. The boy was on his knees, panting closer to the spot of the chief while his face bruised and blood drooling from the side of his mouth. And the big guy was on his knees, on the verge of collapsing.

He could no longer be a spectator, time to act, so he ran and long jumped inside the circle of fire.

"Here," he offered his hand to Renil. The boy looked upwards and met the eyes he thought he would never see again.

A person often meets his destiny on the road he took to avoid it.

"You," he looked puzzled.

"We don't have time for this," the sleuthhound replied, and Renil took his hand. He pulled him back on his feet and the party of two was ready for the rumble, their backs pressed against one another.

The sight was spectacular, both men were short compared to the crowd they were facing, but they were strong. They looked dangerous, the stature and their built were relatively identical, and so their battle stance. One held a jack-knife in his hand and the other had a wooden stick ready for the knockout.

Renil finally realized he was mistaken for the man standing next to him, and everything made perfect sense to him.

On his way through the trail, following the smoke and fire, Joel had seen three men walking away from the dense moors and a body being transported on the shoulders of one of those men, a huge man, the same man who was fighting the boy in the ring of fire but he did not disturb the business, he was not sure who those men were taking with them. He had choked Uliana, thinking she was amongst people from the forest. But before he was about to kill her, she called a name, Renil, and that stopped him. He realized it was the runaway boy who he had seen earlier that evening.

The clouds thundered and beamed with lightning and a sudden neighing of horses, and the shuffling sound of horse's steps followed.

"Hyaah!"

The sound became louder, and the horse steps became clearer as if galloping faster and faster.

Everyone froze at the moment.

From the edge of the Sachem's spot, a voice screamed, "OORSLAAN!"

The horse knew his command well and leapt forward. High and far. The horse landed neatly inside the fire ring and stopped where the men teamed up.

A human figure jumped down from the mighty black horse, drawing a long light-weighted thrusting sword dripping blood of the then chief, Hiute.

Pulling off the hood she took her stance, her untamed hair and aggressive body language boosting the flames to the fire.

She knew why her cottage got set on fire. The tribal thought her to be an ally with the man who had killed their leader, the Horn Head. It was hard to guess the difference between Renil and Joel for the native forest dwellers as both the men were not from the forest and looked quite similar.

The markings from jack-knife of Joel led the party of three to the chalet and they had seen the boy from the window of the cottage, he was alone in the woods, and it was their best chance. So, they shot him with wolf's bane and took him hostage to avenge the slaughter of their father.

But it was too late to sort things out.

The sword had acquainted the blood already.

"Ready for the midnight dance," she asked.

LIX

The moorland had a cold malevolent air to it despite the ring of fire growing loud. The wind howling past in every way, as if trying to express its confusion at the sight.

'Be still,' the wind screamed more than it howled.

The people of the forest seemed to have doubled in numbers suddenly. The gigantic group eyes looked at the triad, suggesting they had no place to hide. It was strange-the air tasted wrong, different and unnatural.

The trio got trapped from all the corners.

Uliana knew they will get mobbed and slaughtered like sheep. They must be quick with the game plan. The only way to keep up is by seeking to circumvent the ring of fire and fleeing on the horsebacks.

The boy had made his mind that he will not run away this time and stand his ground. And the next moment a projectile came flying again from the Sachem spot towards Joel, but before it could hit its target Renil heaved Joel down and he got saved.

The boy in the reflex then stood up and ran towards the beast who was tussling with the aconitum. He picked the blowgun dart and pinned it to the point, the limber neck and gave it a revengeful twist. The needle broke halfway inside the windpipe of Nakoda.

He growled in pain and fell on the ground, instantaneously.

Suddenly mobbed, the fire torches came rushing inside the circle of fire and the triumvirate closed in to take on their enemies.

"We need to hold them only for a brief span and then we will split and divert them," Joel commanded.

The rage of the crowd was that of a Tsunami, the human bodies came in waves and tried to entomb the triad, the circle of fire gave them an edge as the tribal numbers count for nothing because the passage to enter the circle was narrow.

She replied to the sticks with the sword. Uliana was slaying all who tried to attack her.

Renil was spinning the wooden stick made of cedar, using them against the people of the forest, keeping his side of the crowd at bay.

Joel snatched a fire torch and a woodcut stick from his side of attackers and was weaving his moves and burning and stabbing the tribal flesh with exactness.

The air had become hazy, a red mist was thrown up from the sheet of blood that spilt in a relatively short time. The mist and the blue-sky meeting, joining and combining until the sky, the night sky, was auburn, urging the clouds to thunder again.

But the crowd was in no mood to settle and kept hopping the wall of fire.

Molten red blood splashed from the open wounds, mostly from the side Uliana was fighting from, including her own. Her sword was clinking and clashing with folk weapons under the churning sky.

A storm brewed on the cold horizon, promising nothing but rain.

Renil was holding the banging and bashing at his line while the swarm of tribal attacked him, pushing his attacker to the edge of fire leaving them burnt and helpless to retreat, but he was getting weary and tired of the internal wounds from the duel with Nakoda.

Joel was roasting and rupturing the muscles and flesh of the primitive men, and the dewy grass flickered like diamond flames as blood-curdling howl rent the air. However, he had a burn in his gut from the jump he had made to help Renil.

"We must speedily retreat," she shouted.

Joel knew she was right, but the boy, despite being worn out, wanted to fight until his last breath.

She calculated that his emotions were taking a hold of him.

She yelled, "Renil, we must retreat speedily." And now, taken by surprise, she could not bear the assault and her weapon dropped. Before she could find a cover, the tribal-like hound dogs ripped off her cape.

Grey sky restlessly grumbled. It dragged thick blackened clouds down by the heavy rains which remain held in its delicate frame until now. The clouds, which struggled to withstand the burden of the weight which the rain held, soon gave in. The rain poured down over the moorland with a roar.

Everything came to a still in a sixtieth of an hour.

LX

None can harm to whom the God shields.

It is one of the most sought-after stones, deep, celestial blue called lapis. The symbol of royalty and honour, Gods and power, spirit and vision it encourages self-awareness, allows self-expression and shall help reveal an inner truth. It shall provide qualities of honesty, compassion and morality to the personality.

He knelt on the grass, took off the stone he wore, and with his cerulean eyes, he smiled at her. "It belongs to you now," he blessed her before the last knot made on the neck chain, she commemorated, leaving the little stone to rest on her chest, and then he kissed her on her forehead.

"I will always be there with you," he assured her. Secretly he knew his time has come, but being a father is a bigger responsibility than everything else put together.

"We may not stay together, but whenever you want me just touch the lapis and I will be there with you in your heart," the soft voice repeated.

She had lived this moment more than the number of times she can count, but this may be was that one last time.

LXI

The scent was strong and soothing, like when rain falls on dry soil. A soft breeze comforted her head, providing a sweet sensation of rejuvenation. The view in front was quiet and without the fire. The markings on the ground smudged, and the crowd was sitting peacefully waiting for their leader to awake and arise.

It was the Sachem spot, the revamped cedar wooden chair felt beneath and the paddy providing the additional support. A gentle touch helped me sit upright.

A broad smile separated the lips when the source of it got known.

"Are you alright?"

"Yes, I am," She saw Joel.

He could finally connect why the face looked so familiar.

The hood mostly covered the face, but he had seen his master up close and what he saw in Uliana her pronounced features were of fatherly inheritance.

The man who offered guidance to the frail young Joel and the one who became his master was Zephyr.

Clouds behind her, in the background, held a blend of Pyrenees morn, orange, red and violet hues.

Everything at that moment reminded him of his time with his wilding friend Zephyr.

Zephyr visited the abandoned moorland for three full moons, and in one of those seven years, he worked in the neighbouring forest where he had met the young Joel.

"Learn to enjoy the process of the journey as the destination is merely an end. Trust the timings of life and always have faith in what you do. What you wish for is what you find," he repeated the words told by his wildling teacher to her.

The people of the forest found a neck chain on the women they were fighting. The stone in the centre seemed precious, and they took it to the oldest member of their community. He confirmed the chain unmistakably belonged to their ex-chief, Zephyr.

"The best man I had ever known was your father, not mine," a voice from her side commented, offering a hand.

Taking the hand, she met him with humility.

It was the clean-limbed and gracefully thin man named Peroria.

Unlike his brothers, he accepted the lady in the cape as the rightful successor for the people of the forest and apologized for his doings.

"I was simply serving orders from my clan leader," my brother-Hiute.

"We do what we do for our loved ones," she said, forgivingly.

The hide and seek was finally over, and both Joel and Renil were sitting together.

Renil had learnt the art of passively healing the monster within and had changed in ways unimaginable.

What he had done, his past, was a mistake because he only saw things through the lens of his own need. People don't change with time; they change by choice.

She had known him for such a short duration, but she had known him better than anyone else.

Life is from the inside out and when you shift on the inside, life shifts on the outside.

Epilogue

The fields were all around, through the tinted windows. Gazing straight ahead, the world outside continued like some choreographed dance, but without the soul, it should have. While his teal blue sedan raced on the highway.

His phone rang. It was his old friend.

Joel replied, "I'll do it for you."

It was the young man from the family photograph at the duplex who had called, Ervin Victor, son of the provost. He was Joel's employer – his good friend asking for help.

The suspect was the usual sort, the kind that had never had steady or dependable love in their lives, the kind born into cruel chaos that comes on intergenerational trauma.

Renil accepted all the charges put against him except for the murder of his mother. He kept repeating to the attorney, "That was an accident." However, they had him convicted for mass murder, carnage and damaging public property, and he was sentenced to life imprisonment as per the jurisdiction of Radena.

Joel knew the boy was honest about his mother since he had seen her at the cabin, and it was more of a new world problem, the problem of troubled and directionless young people ending up in prisons.

He visited Renil for the next eight years and they became friends as he knew what Renil did was wrong but that is not who he truly is.

During his time in prison, he shared his learning's from the woods which helped felons to behave better and lead a simpler, more meaningful life. Considering his behaviour and little help from Joel he was released on parole after all those long years.

The seventh road still had a Terrace signboard, but it was changed to a fine dining restaurant. He moved away from the parking and towards the road across the parking space which offered a superior view of the landscape.

The Arnnora forest was a warm place, and he was welcomed with songs, hymns and hugs. Greeting the men and women he was escorted to an unchanged Sachem spot. His eyes met with the pair of hazel-coloured eyes, of his love, Uliana.

She was briefing some people when she happened to move her gaze to the man standing at some distance.

"Renil," she spoke in amazement.

Their lips separated into a smile and hearts raced like first time lovers, she came running and kissed him on his lips. He held her in his arms in the moment of joy. The two kept smiling at each other without exchanging a word. Time flies love doesn't. And before they knew everything was happy again, a sense of calm and fulfilment came in.

The stillness broke when he felt something pulling his trousers, looking down he saw the innocent cerulean eyes of a girl, her black hair falling on her forehead.

"Who is this little angel?" he asked earnestly.

"She is our daughter."

The End

www.ingramcontent.com/pod-product-compliance
Lightning Source LLC
LaVergne TN
LVHW091051150826
845673LV00002B/544

* 9 7 9 8 8 8 5 2 1 4 7 8 0 *